Advance Praise for *God's Kingdom*

"This is American fiction at its very best, a rip-roaring story full of hilarity and heartbreak. I finished it feeling better about myself and life in general. *God's Kingdom* is the good stuff, the very best stuff, honest and emotionally resonant. Don't miss it." —Stephen King

"It's impossible to read *God's Kingdom* without thinking of Mark Twain on every page, because in this lovely, moving book Howard Frank Mosher strikes that same Manichaean balance between deep misgivings about the "damned human race" and equally profound affection for individual men and women. Over the years Mosher's beloved Vermont "Kingdom" has become one of America's most magical literary places."
—Richard Russo, Pulitzer Prize–winning
author of *Empire Falls*

"With *God's Kingdom*, Howard Frank Mosher has delivered a powerful and striking tale of family and place and of how deeply intertwined the two can be—a sense of a vanishing America but truly a rural America that is familiar in tone if not detail to us all. Mosher's keen wit and gentle sense of the absurdity of life is fully present but also a telling examination of the secrets that bind and can also splinter a family. The ghosts of history, alongside a landscape that appears to nurture, while in fact being careless of our existence, run side by side throughout the novel and in the end, we are left with the

pause of beauty, the moment of grace, the relentless swelling of hope. A rare achievement in contemporary American letters."
—Jeffrey Lent, author of *In the Fall*

"Howard Frank Mosher is an American treasure in the long or short form, or any hybrid between. And guess what: he keeps getting better."
—Tom Franklin, author of *Crooked Letter, Crooked Letter*

"We are just plain lucky that Howard Frank Mosher has written so deeply and in the end invented Vermont, this version, so far north that the border runs through it; and he is able in this rich coming-of-age story to invoke the humane spirit of Sherwood Anderson, who had his own kingdom in Winesburg. This love letter to the North Country brims with the profound natural world and peels back layers of the personal mysteries imbedded in its history. *God's Kingdom* held me to the last page."
—Ron Carlson, author of *Return to Oakpine*

"This irresistible novel should bring Howard Frank Mosher the big audience his work deserves. Reading *God's Kingdom* is like listening to a masterful storyteller around the fire. There's a man named Moose with a pet moose, an inspiring mute, a brilliant former slave, a basketball phenom named Crazy, a Pulitzer-winning curmudgeon, and a spinster who sees the future. These bighearted stories build artfully upon each other. And along the way, Mosher invents—and often kills— more unforgettable characters in one sprawling family in one slender novel than most writers create in a lifetime. His quirky imagined world is tinged with whimsy and magic yet utterly convincing, as if these pages sprang from the soil of northern Vermont."　　　　　—Jim Lynch, author of *The Highest Tide* and *Truth Like the Sun*

"*God's Kingdom* is a pleasure and a surprise. It has everything one would expect from a Howard Mosher novel and a lot more, too. It is fun to read, and is filled with adventures, beguiling characters, the presence of the natural world and its beauties; but it is also compelling evidence that Howard Mosher has really just begun. This, I think, is his best book, but that is only because it is his most recent. If you have not read Mosher, the loss is yours. If you have, more pleasure is on the way."

　　　　　—Craig Nova, author of *The Good Son*

"In *God's Kingdom* Mosher brings us the coming of age of a young writer; along the way we see the kingdom as Jimmy sees it, its harshness, as well as its glory, and through the good, the bad, and the ugly is the triumph of the human spirit and the benediction of the landscape upon that spirit. *God's Kingdom* is one of those fictions that leave the reader uplifted without sacrificing truth, realism, or style."

　　　　　—Ernest Hebert, author of the Darby Chronicles

"In *God's Kingdom*, Howard Frank Mosher again displays the qualities that make him the nonpareil chronicler of a vanishing upcountry New England. The author's deep knowledge of, and affection for, his landscape and its denizens resonates in every sentence of this bright new novel. Mosher's work is regional, yes, but only in the sense that Robert Frost's was: his deep contemplation of local matters provides a lens through which he and his lucky reader can more keenly know what it is to be human." —Sydney Lea, Poet Laureate of Vermont and author of *A North Country Life*

"Howard Frank Mosher's stunning new novel, *God's Kingdom*, begins as a coming-of-age story, and ends up an epic work of genius. Not since Hemingway's Nick Adams has there been a character so expertly and lovingly written as Jim Kinneson. For decades in his indispensable novels, Howard Frank Mosher has refracted Vermont's Northeast Kingdom into historical precincts of stark reality, composed hardscrabble human music, drawn landscapes seemingly seanced up from before the Age of Reason, and played out Fate like slowly building storms in his character's hearts. He is the rarest thing in literature: an original. Vermont is Mr. Mosher's literary kingdom and he rules it with a bittersweet pen pressed hard to the page."

—Howard Norman, author of *Next Life Might Be Kinder*

"Few writers plumb the cords that link fathers and sons with the hope—and humor—of Howard Frank Mosher. He is wistful and wise, and his moral compass is as precise as his immense skills as a storyteller. I cherish my visits to the mythical Kingdom County that once upon a time was Vermont."

—Chris Bohjalian, author of *The Sandcastle Girls* and *Close Your Eyes, Hold Hands*

GOD'S
KINGDOM

GOD'S KINGDOM

Howard Frank Mosher

St. Martin's Press

New York

GOD'S KINGDOM. Copyright © 2015 by Howard Frank Mosher. All rights reserved. Printed in the United States of America. For information, address St. Martin's Press, 175 Fifth Avenue, New York, N.Y. 10010.

www.stmartins.com

Chapter 2, "White Knights" was originally published in *Hunger Mountain Review,* in 2013, in a somewhat different format.

The Library of Congress Cataloging-in-Publication Data is available upon request.

ISBN 978-1-250-06948-1 (hardcover)
ISBN 978-1-4668-8200-3 (e-book)

St. Martin's Press books may be purchased for educational, business, or promotional use. For information on bulk purchases, please contact the Macmillan Corporate and Premium Sales Department at 1-800-221-7945, extension 5442, or write to specialmarkets@macmillan.com.

First Edition: October 2015

10 9 8 7 6 5 4 3 2 1

To Phillis
aka
Dr. Frannie Lafleur Kinneson

GOD'S
KINGDOM

1

Blooded

On the earliest maps of Vermont, the wilderness that would later become Kingdom County was referred to as "Territory but Little Known." The first settlers called it "God's Kingdom," in reference to its remoteness and extraordinary beauty. To this day, you will occasionally hear the term "God's Kingdom" used to suggest the wild and unspoiled character of this last New England frontier.

—THE REVEREND DR. PLINY TEMPLETON,
*The Ecclesiastical, Natural, Social, and Political History
of Kingdom County*

In those years in God's Kingdom there was always a ridge runner. There was always one deer that was bigger, darker, and smarter, with ten or more points on its antlers and a track three fingers wide and as deep as the snow was soft. Of course, there was more snow then. Back when Editor James Kinneson was just Jimmy Kinneson, a boy who had not yet been blooded, it seemed that by Thanksgiving week at the latest there was always a foot of fresh snow in the Kingdom.

The year Jim turned fourteen they referred to the ridge

runner as "Jimmy's deer." "That old boy has your name on him, bub," Jim's older brother, Charlie, told him. It was as though Charlie, and Jim's grandfather and namesake, James Kinneson II, and Jim's father, Editor Charles Kinneson, had let the runner grow to a great size so that it would be there for Jim to hunt when he turned fourteen. This was the usual age for a boy to be blooded in the Kingdom of that era.

They left for camp on Thanksgiving Day after the big meal at the Kinneson family farmhouse, heading up along the river toward the Canadian border in Charlie's pickup. Their gear was in the bed of the truck. The open-sighted .30-30 deer rifles they favored in the dense woods on the mountain. Their sleeping bags. An extra set of clothing. "Go light—the lighter the better," was Gramp's hunting motto. Gramp was already at the camp. Charlie and the editor and Jim would meet him there.

As they bounced up the washboard road along the river toward the border, Charlie's empties rolled around on the towing chain under Jim's feet, clattering together like little glass duckpins.

"My God, Charles, you ought to hoe out your rig once every decade or so," the editor said.

"Why?" Charlie said. "I'm just going to give it to Jim when he turns sixteen. He can hoe it out then."

The road ended in a brushy clearing, beyond which the river widened into Pond Number One. The camp boat, a former lumbering bateau painted dark green, sat upside down under a tarp in a stand of black spruce on the shore. They transferred their gear from the truck bed to the boat and started out across the open water. Charlie rowed, the editor sat in the squared-off stern, Jim sat facing backward in the bow. The surface of Pond Number One was calm and the same steel gray as their rifle barrels.

Jim was excited by the prospect of hunting the ridge runner. He'd glimpsed it this past August when he and Gramp were fishing Pond Number One from Gramp's Old Town. They'd spotted the buck drinking from the pond near the collapsing logging dam across the outlet. Except for a white patch on its chest, it was as red in its summer coat as a Jersey cow, and its horns were in velvet. Jim counted six points on each side. The deer lifted its head and watched them for a moment as water slid off its dark muzzle into the pond. Then it made two long bounds and vanished into the woods. Gramp looked at Jim and nodded. That was all. But Jim knew that this was the ridge runner. Come hunting season, if he was smart enough to walk it down and shoot it, this was his deer.

They put out just above the dam spillway where Jim and Gramp had seen the runner the past summer, and dragged the heavy bateau around the broken-down old dam and put it back into the rippling, noisy current, which carried them fast down the river to Pond Number Two. Charlie would have shipped his oars and shot the spillway in the bateau had he and Jim been alone. Gramp, too, liked to shoot the spillway. But the editor was all about boat safety and water safety, not to mention gun safety, and disapproved of taking any risks whatsoever on the water or in the woods.

Soon the river slowed down and opened out into Pond Number Two. The fishing here was never as good as the fishing in Number One except once in a cloudburst when Jim and Gramp couldn't distinguish between the surface of the pond and the torrents of water pouring out of the sky and trout were rising to their flies so fast that it seemed to be raining fish.

There was no dam at the outlet of Pond Number Two. It had gone out with the ice in a spring freshet decades ago. Just another short stretch of quick water, then Pond Number Three, then the rapids, then the Dead Water between Kingdom and Canada Mountains and, beyond the Dead Water, the big lake, Memphremagog, stretching twenty-five miles across the border into Canada through mountains taller still.

Out on the ponds in the bateau no one spoke much, even Charlie. It was fall-still on the flat open water. The water dripping off the oars and the occasional muffled *thunk* of an oar blade bumping the wooden side of the bateau was the only sounds this late in the year. Even the pair of loons that raised a brood on Pond Number Three every summer was gone. Jim looked back over his shoulder. The tops of Kingdom and Canada Mountains were invisible in the clouds. Smoke curled out of the black stovepipe of the camp at the foot of Kingdom Mountain. Gramp stood on the pebbly shore next to the green, canvas-covered Old Town, watching as the bateau drew closer.

"I thought the *loup-garou* had gotten you boys," Gramp said, grabbing the bow of the bateau and pulling it grating up onto the pebbles. "Did you bring along some of that Thanksgiving turkey? For camp meat?"

This was one of Gramp's standard jokes. He supplied the camp meat himself. By the time Jim and his dad and brother arrived at camp, Gramp always had a young doe hanging from the game beam. In those years there was no doe season in Vermont, but Gramp said that God's Kingdom wasn't in Vermont, or in Canada, either. Gramp said that the Kingdom belonged to God. As with the Sabbath, God had created deer for the benefit of mankind, not the other way around.

Jim helped carry the rifles and gear up the slope to the camp. Long ago some Kinneson ancestor had carved the words "God's Kingdom" on the lintel over the door. Jim had never been sure whether "God's Kingdom" referred to the hunting camp or the territory they hunted.

In the hour before supper Charlie walked up the mountain to scout for sign. While Jim's father and grandfather cut up the doe, Jim read in the camp journal, a tall ledger-book with blank white pages where, for one hundred and fifty years, Kinnesons had recorded the weather, seasons, game hunted, fish caught, and visitors to the camp.

Abenaki fur trader, Sabattis, stopped for night en route to Montreal. C. Kinneson, April 3, 1801.

Sighted 6 caribou-deer on ice on Two at sunset. J. Kinneson, January 26, 1815.

And, from the past summer, Jim's single entry:

Spotted huge red buck, 12 points, near dam of Two at sunset. J. Kinneson III, August 10, 1952.

Jim's father liked to say that while Gramp ran the camp, he ran the frying pan. As he fried up venison tenderloins, the editor said, "How many points did this young skipper have, Dad?"

"What, you eat the horns, do you, Charles?" Gramp said, winking at Jim.

Jim grinned. He knew what was coming next.

"If this deer had horns, I'll eat them," the editor said.

The camp door opened and a gust of wind and snow blew in with Charlie. "He's been up there, Jimmy. Your runner. I found his rubs on a young maple. I saw some fresh tracks, too. Headed down toward the cedar swamp along the Dead Water."

"I could have told you all that this afternoon when you arrived, Charlie," Gramp said. "I believe young Jim is going to have a good hunt tomorrow."

"If he doesn't get buck fever and hurry his shot," Charlie said, elbowing Jim.

"Let's eat," Gramp said. "Jim isn't going to get buck fever. Are you, Jimmy?"

"No," Jim said, wishing he had as much confidence in himself as Gramp seemed to have in him.

After supper Jim cleared the table. Charlie heated water in the tin dishpan and washed the dishes as Jim rinsed them with cold water from the hand pump in the wooden sink. Jim liked doing camp chores with his brother. Like their father, the editor, Charlie was tall, six feet two or three. Jim hoped that someday he'd be tall, too, but for his age he was slight, and seemed to favor Gramp instead. Of the three living generations of

Kinneson men, Gramp was the best hunter. Even Jim's dad said so. The editor said that Gramp was the best man in the woods in all Kingdom County, and the best storyteller, as well.

Gramp settled into his white-ash old-man's rocker beside the Glenwood. The editor sat at the table, noting the day's weather in the camp journal. Jim and Charlie played King of the Mountain for the choice perch on the lid of the woodbox. After a tussle, Charlie let Jim win. Picking himself up off the floor and laughing, Jim's brother sat down at the table across from the editor.

"I noticed you reading the camp log before supper, Jimmy," Gramp said.

"Yes, sir," Jim said. "They didn't shoot many deer up here in the early years, did they?"

"There weren't many deer to shoot," Gramp said. "There were very few natural meadows for deer to graze in. Just un-broken woods when the first Kinneson came here. That would have been your great-great-great-grandfather Charles I. He came here to hunt men, not deer."

Gramp never hurried a story. After a pause he said, "Charles Kinneson I was born in Scotland. He fought at Culloden with the Bonnie Prince in the uprising of 1745. After the battle he fled to America and settled in Massachusetts. He first came to Vermont in 1759 with Robert Rogers's Rangers. They were on their way north to Canada, on what they called a retalia-tory raid against the St. Francis Indians."

Gramp looked at Jim to make sure he was listening. The only sound in the camp was the low ticking of the fire in the Glenwood.

"Four miles west of here, where the river empties into the big lake, Rogers's advance scouts came across a small band of Memphremagog Abenakis drying salmon on wooden racks. The Rangers bided their time. Come nightfall, they formed a human chain, crossed the rapids, and crept up on the Indian encampment. According to Charles I, the Memphremagogs were 'holding high frolic' around their campfires, dancing and celebrating. The Rangers caught them unawares and slaughtered every last man, woman, and child."

Jim's father closed the camp journal. "That was a long time ago, Dad," he said. "It happened and it was a terrible thing. But times have changed, thankfully."

The editor gave Gramp a look Jim couldn't read, but Gramp continued his story. "Charles I reported, Jimmy, that some of the Rangers cut off the heads of the murdered Indians and played at tenpins with them. Finally, Major Rogers made them stop."

"Jesus, Dad," the editor said. "We don't know that for a fact. Jimmy doesn't need to hear that."

Charlie winked at Jim. "I wonder what they used for pins?" he said.

"Who's telling this story, gentlemen, me or you?" Gramp said.

"The story's over," the editor said. "It's pretty much the story of the settling of America, and thank Jesus, it's over."

"Not quite," Gramp said. "Some years later, Charles I returned here. He married a Memphremagog woman named Molly Molasses and became the first white settler in God's

Kingdom. He said he settled here to do penance for killing the Indians."

"If so, he could scarcely have picked a better purgatory," Jim's dad said. "This was the end of the known world in those days. 'Territory but Little Known,' they called it."

"Actually," Gramp said, "Charles I built a trading post and a whiskey distillery at the mouth of the river and became quite wealthy."

"That's a good way to do penance," Charlie said. "I wouldn't mind doing penance by getting rich."

They all laughed, and Jim felt relieved because he did not like tension in the family, even when some of it was just joking.

"What do you say, boys?" Gramp said, standing up. "If we're going to tumble out early tomorrow morning and get this young fella blooded, we'd better tumble in now. Hop down, Jimmy. Time to bank the ashes."

Jim jumped down off the woodbox lid and Gramp got a chunk of yellow birch and put it in the Glenwood's firebox and raked coals and ashes over it. The burning birch bark gave off a wintergreen fragrance. Jim could still smell the sweet scent a few minutes later from the camp loft, where he lay in his sleeping bag in the darkness, waiting to fall asleep, waiting for morning to arrive.

That night Jim stayed awake in the dark a long time, too excited about hunting the ridge runner the next day to sleep. He thought of the years he'd spent practicing. The training started about the time he began school. He and Gramp would go out to the maple orchard behind the farmhouse after a snowfall. Gramp would hand Jim his gold pocket watch. "A quarter of an hour," he'd say. Then he'd head up the slope into the maples.

Fifteen interminable minutes later Jim would start out after his grandfather, following his boot prints in the snow. Gramp would be waiting for him on the upper edge of the sugar bush. "Good hunt," he'd tell Jimmy.

A couple of years later they began tracking on bare ground. At first Gramp left plenty of sign. Broken branches, wet spots on stepping-stones in the brook. Later the tracking got tougher. A single heel mark in a wet meadow, bent-back blades of marsh grass, jittery crows over a copse of balsam fir trees. Once Jim came to a hillside where Gramp's footprints in a dusting of new snow stopped as though he'd been snatched from the face of the earth by a flying saucer. It had taken Jim a long time to figure out that Gramp had walked backward in his own tracks, stepped off into the brook, cut back down the slope in the water, and slipped in behind him.

That was the fall Gramp began taking Jim to the woods with a gun. At ten Jim wasn't allowed to carry the gun, just to accompany Gramp while he walked down a deer. Gramp could track a deer over bare ledge or through the worst cedar jungle. He knew where and when a deer would take to deep water to elude a hunter, when a buck sought high ground instead. He told Jim that over a short distance a deer could outrun a racehorse. But a man had much more endurance than any deer, and could think, besides. If a man used his head, he could always walk down his deer.

Summer evenings Gramp taught Jim to shoot in the meadow beside the farmhouse. They started with a single-shot .22. When Jim was eleven, he began going with Gramp for grouse and ducks with a sixteen gauge. At twelve he learned how to shoot Gramp's .30-30. Once he heard Gramp tell Dad, "The boy is an accurate shot and noticing in the woods." For his age, Gramp said, Jim was as good as the best. Lying in the camp loft, Jim thought that he and Gramp might get their woods sense from Molly Molasses and her Abenaki ancestors. He liked thinking that his original Kingdom forbears were Indians. He did not like to think about Charles I and the other Rangers slaughtering the Memphremagog Abenakis and bowling with their heads.

Jim's dad was always trying to get Gramp to write down his stories, even if the editor didn't entirely approve of Gramp's telling Jim every last gruesome detail. Gramp said he'd leave it to Jim to write the stories of the Kingdom. At fourteen, Jim had already begun to. Now he decided that when he wrote Charles I's story, he would put in the part about the Rangers playing at tenpins with the severed heads. It was both the worst and best part of the story.

This was Jim Kinneson's last thought before drifting off to sleep in God's Kingdom, up in the little-known mountains of northern Vermont hard by the Canadian border.

Clang clang clang clang.

Gramp was beating on the bottom of the dishpan with a spoon. "Wake up, boy. Tumble up, roll out," he called up to Jim. Then the old breakfast joke: "If we had some ham, we could have ham and eggs—if we had some eggs."

They did have ham and eggs, and Mom's homemade bread toasted over an open lid of the Glenwood, and fried potatoes, and tinned prunes since Gramp was a great hand at making sure everyone stayed regular at camp. All washed down with the editor's famous camp coffee: three heaping handfuls of freshly ground coffee thrown in the blue porcelain coffeepot with a broken eggshell to settle the grounds.

Gramp and Jim headed out at first light. They stopped on the edge of the big cedars beside the Dead Water to watch the eastern sky turn pink. Kingdom and Canada Mountains loomed high above the flow. Fifty years ago the Great North Woods Timber Company had erected a long earthen dam across the mouth of the river, flooding out the rapids and creating the deep flow known as the Dead Water in order to prevent logs from jamming up in the notch during the spring drives.

"Walk up through the cedars along the edge of the Dead Water," Gramp said. "You should jump him someplace between here and the notch. Don't push him too hard at first. You don't want to panic him into swimming across the flow into Canada. If you run into trouble or need help dragging him out, fire three shots ten seconds apart. Wait twenty minutes and do it again."

Gramp handed Jim his watch. They stood together near the edge of the water, watching the color in the east bleed higher up the sky, as if in defiance of gravity. "All right, then," Gramp said. "Have a good hunt."

Gramp headed back toward the camp, moving in easy, even strides. Ahead, the reflection of the sunrise glowed crim-

son on the granite wall of Kingdom Mountain. Jim checked
his rifle to make sure the safety was on. Then he started into
the cedars. The flow crawled along through the swamp,
bloodred in the spreading sunrise.

Jim cut the runner's track twenty minutes later. He'd expected it to be impressively big, but when he first saw the
deer's prints in the snow under the cedars he thought they
might belong to a moose. At the foot of the twin cliffs, where
the dammed-up Dead Water passed through the notch, the
deer had angled back up Kingdom Mountain on an ancient
game trail. The wind was quartering from Jim toward the
ridge runner. That was what he wanted. He wanted the big
buck to know that he was on its trail, as long as he didn't panic
it into going to water and vanishing into Canada.

    Partway up the mountain, in a former log landing growing
up to wild raspberries, the game trail forked. The more-traveled
branch ran straight up over the mountain past the Balance
Boulder. A lesser-used trace angled off to the south, travers-
ing the mountainside high above the three ponds. The runner
had taken the south branch.

    Jim knew this side of the mountain well from partridge
hunting here with Gramp, and berrying in the summertime.
It was steep and ledgy, with stiff, gray-green caribou moss
growing on the floor of the forest. Twice that morning, from
far off to the south, he heard the echoing boom of some other
hunter's rifle. While the ridge runner was now heading away
from the flow and Canada, it occurred to Jim that he might

drive the deer out of the woods in front of a weekend hunter like the down-country sports who stayed at the Common Hotel and ventured out to road hunt for a few hours in the middle of the day, hoping for a lucky shot at something with horns that they could put on the wall back home. When the runner turned off the game trail and headed down the snowy mountainside toward Pond Number Two, far from the lumber roads cruised by the weekend hunters, Jim was relieved.

It began to snow. The buck had turned back to the north again, seeking shelter in a thick stand of black spruce trees between Two and Three. Jim came to a deer yard where the runner's tracks mingled with the prints of other deer. Twice he lost its trail and had to backtrack. Even so, he was gaining on the animal. He picked up its deep tracks again along the boggy southern margin of Number Three. Here the two-pronged impressions were so recent that groundwater was still oozing into them. The water reminded Jim that he needed to drink more. He refilled his canteen from an icy rill coming off the mountainside. Nearby, he came to a place where the deer had lain down beside a brush pile. It was time to begin pushing the tiring buck. Jim checked the .30-30 to make sure that the safety was still on. Then he began to trot.

The deer surprised Jim by passing less than a hundred yards behind the hunting camp, which sat empty-looking, its stovepipe smokeless, on the slope above Three. His grandfather and father and brother were miles away, each one looking for his own deer. They might not be back at camp until long after dark.

Near the raspberry brake where the trail forked, the ridge runner had crossed the tracks of a smaller deer, a yearling doe or a young spikehorn. Ordinarily, a mature buck in rut would follow the smaller track, to breed the doe or chase off the spike. Not today. Today, knowing that it was being hunted, Jim's deer took the trail up the mountain toward the timberline.

On the edge of the tree line, just below the height of land, the deer had collapsed again in a miniature forest of ancient, wind-twisted spruce and fir trees no higher than Jim's knees. As he approached, it sprang up and went crashing through the snow, its tail flashing like a white flag waved in surrender. But the runner was not yet ready to give up.

The mountaintop above the timberline was strewn with mossy boulders. The largest of these was the almost perfectly round Balance Boulder, a huge glacial erratic. To Jim it looked like a gigantic, dark bowling ball. The runner was standing at the base of the great round boulder, its legs trembling from fear or exhaustion or both. In the westering sun, hazy through a film of crystalline snowflakes, the animal was as red as it had been in its summer coat when Jim and Gramp had come upon it drinking from the pond back in August. One of its antler points had been snapped off, probably in combat with another buck. The runner squatted and peed nervously, its legs shaking, as Jim slowly approached it.

Jim raised his rifle. His hands on the stock and trigger guard were as steady as the granite outcropping on the mountaintop. His heartbeat seemed to slow as he thumbed off the safety. Before the boy knew he was going to do it, he lowered the rifle. He thumbed on the safety and jacked each of the five brass-jacketed shells out of the chamber onto the mossy rocks at his feet.

The deer stood motionless as Jim raised the rifle again, flipped off the safety, aimed at the animal's chest, and pressed the trigger. On the silent mountaintop in the sunset, the *click* of the firing pin falling on the empty chamber sounded louder than it was. Jim lowered his gun and took a few steps and the ridge runner was gone, off down the far side of the mountain toward the big lake where Jim's Abenaki ancestors had once fished for salmon. Jim thought about the Indians celebrating their catch by firelight, unaware of Charles I and the Rangers crossing the rapids just upriver. As the sun rested on the peaks far to the west, and the Balance Boulder glowed red in its reflection, Jim turned to head back down the mountain, and saw Gramp standing behind him in the clearing, the unspent shells from Jim's rifle gleaming in his hand.

On the way down the mountainside in the snowy dusk, they jumped a spikehorn stripping the bark from a moose maple, and Jim shot it cleanly through the heart. Probably it was the same young deer whose tracks he'd cut late that afternoon in the raspberry brake.

"Well, son," the editor said when Jim and Gramp dragged the spike into the camp yard at twilight, "that young skipper wasn't what you were looking for, but it will get you blooded just as quickly."

"Don't feel bad, bub," Charlie said. "Your runner isn't going anywhere. He'll be there for you next year."

"He made a fine, running shot on the spike," Gramp said. "No buck fever. I call this a good hunt."

In the morning Charlie and the editor hunted the edge of the Dead Water for a few hours. Jim and Gramp caught a mess of out-of-season trout for chowder. Jim split wood and filled the woodbox for whoever came to God's Kingdom next. He recorded his deer in the camp journal:

Shot a spikehorn on Kingdom Mountain. J. Kinneson III, Nov. 28, 1952.

That afternoon Charlie rowed the editor across the three ponds in the bateau. Gramp and Jim paddled out behind them in the Old Town. The spike lay in the bottom of the canoe, its head lolling over the gunnel. Jim hadn't mentioned the ridge runner and neither had Gramp. What had taken place on the mountaintop would remain there.

It was snowing again when they reached Charlie's rig, the flakes beginning to collect on the spike's dark winter coat. Jim rode in back with his deer and the Old Town.

Snow was still falling that evening when Charlie and Gramp and the editor drove Jim and his deer around the village green three times in Charlie's truck, horn honking, in a procession of half a dozen other pickups carrying boys who had shot their first deer and been blooded by the oldest hunter in their family. Gramp had dipped his index and middle fingers into the cut in the spike's throat where they'd bled it out and painted

two stripes down Jim's cheeks and two more across his forehead. Jim felt proud and a little self-conscious to be paraded
around the green. He hoped that, in the years to come, he
would have many more good hunts in God's Kingdom with his
grandfather and father and brother, but he knew in his heart
that this would be the last deer he would ever kill.

2

White Knights

During the War Between the States, we sometimes amused our-
selves with a version of One Old Cat we called "Base-ball." I
later introduced the game to Kingdom Common, where we cre-
ated what I believe was the first baseball "diamond" in New
England.

—PLINY TEMPLETON

The Knights need a teetotaler driver tomorrow, Jimbo,"
Harlan Kittredge said. "Are you a teetotaler?"

It was the evening of June 20. Tomorrow the White Knights
of Temperance, formerly the Kingdom County Outlaws, were
headed to Boston to catch the twin bill between the Sox and
the Yankees. They'd gotten together tonight at the Common
Hotel to put the finishing touches on their plans for the trip.

At fifteen, Jim Kinneson, the Knights' shortstop and leadoff hitter, was the team's youngest player. Unsure what a teetotaler was, Jim looked over the top of his orange Nehi at his
older brother, Charlie, for assistance. Charlie was ogling Miss
Pinky, the girl singer in the hotel band. A cat-eyed crooner out

of Breaux Bridge, Louisiana, with a voice like a rusty yard pump, Miss Pinky could belt out "If You've Got the Money, Honey" loudly enough to be heard all the way from the hotel barroom to the United Church at the far end of the village green. For months Charlie had been begging her to accompany him on an all-expenses-paid romantic weekend in Montreal. In fact, the entire baseball team was in love with Pinky. Jim was infatuated with her himself.

At present Miss Pinky and her fiddle player were taping a cardboard sign over the bar. It said, "We Still Love You, Hank." Miss P had hand-lettered it with a red crayon in tribute to the late, great Hank Williams, who, at just twenty-nine, had died this past New Year's Day. That was the day the Outlaws had taken the pledge and changed the team's name. Right here in the hotel barroom, with Armand St. Onge, the proprietor, as a witness, the boys had raised their right hands and solemnly sworn to let the hard stuff alone for an entire year. Beer was still permissible. It was a well-known fact, at least to the Knights, that you couldn't become an alkie like Hank on beer. Even Armand said so and he should know. Armand drank two six-packs of Black Label every weeknight and three apiece on Saturday and Sunday.

Still, suds and long-distance driving didn't mix. If the Knights were to get to Boston tomorrow, they needed a sober driver. Jim didn't drink beer or hard stuff. According to Charlie, the team's attorney and catcher, the fact that Jim didn't have his driver's license yet was immaterial. Like most other teenagers in the Kingdom, Jim had been driving for years.

Miss P shimmied her way over to Jim and Charlie's table and shut one eye and surveyed the "We Still Love You, Hank" sign to see if it was plumb. She had long dark hair down her back and a complexion the color of Armand's black-cherry bar. She was tall and slender and sang with a Cajun accent. The fact that she was the only Yankees fan in Kingdom Common made her even more exotic.

Armand stepped up to the microphone. "Ladies and gentlemen," he said, "straight from the Lou'siane bayou, Mademoiselle Pinky, dark as chocolate and just as sweet."

Pinky rolled her eyes as the boys hooted and stomped. The fiddler played a bar of "Jole Blon" while she adjusted the mic.

"Listen, all y'all," Pinky croaked in a voice like a swamp bittern. "Whichever one you *alkies* bring me back a baseball signed by Joe DiMaggio, I'll take you up on that weekend in Montreal."

She pointed a long finger straight at Jim and winked. "That include you, hotshot."

Snub-nosed and hunch-shouldered, the team bus sat in the hotel parking lot in the mountain dawn. It had formerly belonged to an automobile junkyard dealer from Pond in the Sky whom Charlie had gotten off the hook for possession of stolen property. The dealer had paid Charlie in kind with the property in question. The words "Burlington Transit Company" could still be faintly discerned on the side of the bus where the junkyard owner had tried to sand them off.

Harlan Kittredge had painted the team's new name just be-low the imperfectly deleted "Burlington Transit Company." In fire-engine-red letters a foot high Harlan had inscribed the words "White Nights of Temprance." Someone, probably Charlie, had added an inebriated-looking "K" in front of "Nights." No one had bothered to correct the "Temprance."

The bus had a new name of its own: the Ark of the Covenant. It had been conferred by Charlie in commemoration of the vow the boys had made to leave the hard stuff alone.

They headed out just after five A.M. Jim had been practicing for the trip by driving the Ark to away games. Shifting through its six forward gears was the biggest challenge. "Shift!" the boys hollered as the Ark headed south between the village green and the brick shopping block. Jim mashed down on the metal clutch pedal and ratcheted up the floor shift to the next gear.

At the end of the brick block, Jim's dad, Editor Charles Kinneson, was unlocking the door of *The Kingdom County Monitor*. He glanced over his shoulder at the bus but didn't wave. The editor was down on the Sox because they hadn't yet broken the color barrier in Boston by signing on a Negro player. Neither, for that matter, had the Yankees. Jim's dad hadn't told him that he couldn't go to Boston with the Knights, but Jim knew that he didn't approve of the trip.

Jim's only disappointment was that he would miss seeing Ted Williams play. Ted was serving his country in Korea. Seeing Joe DiMaggio would be the next best thing, even if he was a damn Yankee. In Jim's jacket pocket was a brand-new, official American League baseball Charlie'd given him for his fifteenth birthday. If they arrived at Fenway in time for batting practice, Joltin' Joe might sign Jim's baseball for Miss Pinky.

At the south edge of town, just before the dead man's curve and the junction with U.S. Route 5, the "Welcome to Kingdom Common" sign stood shrouded in mist off the Lower Kingdom River. *Good*, Jim thought, as he shifted down for the hairpin bend. He detested the welcome sign, which went on to proclaim, in tall black letters, "Home of the Kingdom Common Academy Catamounts, 1947 Division Four State Baseball Runners-up." As though to notify all visitors to the Common, and remind villagers on a daily basis, that the Academy teams hadn't won any title at all for six years and even then the baseball team had just been runners-up, and in lowly Division IV at that. This coming season, Jim thought. This coming season, the following season at the latest, that was going to change.

Again Jim shifted down, and the ancient transit bus shuddered as it started into the sharp curve. This past New Year's Day, after word of Hank Williams's death had come through to the Common, Charlie and Harlan Kittredge had decided to race their pickups to Hank's funeral in Montgomery, Alabama. Whoever reached Montgomery first would win a one-hundred-dollar pot, to be put up by the other boys on their baseball team. Harlan and Charlie had gotten just this far, the dead man's curve, before the race ended unceremoniously, in an eight-foot snowbank, less than a quarter of a mile from their starting point in the hotel parking lot.

Jim's brother and Harlan had been fortunate. Over the years there had been several bad wrecks at the curve. A decade ago, a carload of kids from the Academy, returning from a drinking binge across the border in Canada, had skidded into the dead man's curve from Route 5 at a high rate of speed. They'd hit black ice and rolled off into the river. Three of the young people had been killed, including a second cousin of Jim and Charlie's. Going drinking at roadhouses across the border was a rite of passage during Jim's youth. Even after the three fatalities at the dead man's curve, local parents tended to look the other way when it came to underage drinking. After all, they'd gone drinking to Canada themselves when they were teenagers. How could they tell their kids not to?

A mile south of town, the long-abandoned Water of Life whiskey distillery slumped into an overgrown field between the Boston and Montreal railroad tracks and the Lower Kingdom River. The roofs of the malting sheds had collapsed. The whiskey-barrel mill beside the penstock on the river looked as though it might topple into the river at any moment. Jim's great-great-great-grandfather Charles Kinneson I had brought the family recipe for the Water of Life whiskey to America from Scotland. For decades before the Civil War the Kinnesons had used every penny from their distillery to support the cause of abolition, but despite the humanitarian purpose to which the proceeds were put, Jim's father, Editor Kinneson, blamed the astronomical present-day rate of alcoholism in God's Kingdom squarely on the family business. As the editor pointed out, it was Kinneson whiskey that Charles I's Rangers had drunk before massacring the Abenaki fishing party and cutting off their heads. Then, of course, there was the sipping perquisite. Pliny Templeton had written about it in his *Ecclesiastical and Natural History*. In accordance with this privilege, workers at the distillery and barrel factory were allowed a dram of whiskey before starting work in the morning, another at noon, and yet another at the end of the day. Also they enjoyed the perquisite of sipping, while at work, all the raw whiskey they could hold and still complete their task. Dad said that even after Prohibition came in and the distillery finally shut its doors, as much illegal whiskey was made in God's Kingdom as in any remote hollow of Kentucky or West Virginia.

Fifteen minutes later, Jim headed south out of the Landing along Lake Kingdom. Lake Kingdom was sometimes known as Runaway Lake. Lying in a five-mile-long glacial bowl on the height of land dividing the St. Lawrence and Connecticut River watersheds, the lake had originally drained south to St. Johnsbury, then into the Connecticut and, eventually, Long Island Sound. At just eighteen years old, Jim's great-grandfather Charles Kinneson II had undertaken, with a crew of men from the distillery, well lubricated with hundred-and-ten-proof Water of Life, to dig a new outlet through a huge natural sand dike at the opposite, *north* end of Lake Kingdom. Charles's design was to increase the flow of water through the penstock of the whiskey-barrel factory on the Lower Kingdom River, which dwindled to little more than a brook nearly every summer. The ensuing flood, when they breached the natural dam, washed away, besides the first distillery and the barrel mill, several farmsteads in the Lower Kingdom Valley. The green in Kingdom Common lay under

six feet of water, and the Landing, then located at the original outlet at the south end of the lake, was left with no water
power to turn its half dozen gristmills and sawmills. Some of
the buildings—the livery, the hotel, the one-room school, and
several houses—were jacked onto rafts and winched up the
lake to the new outlet at the north end. But the townspeople
and millers of Kingdom Landing never did get over their
anger toward Charles II, and the Common, for stranding
their town high and dry, and the animosity between the two
villages had continued to simmer up to the present.

As the bus crested the height of land and started down the
long slope toward St. Johnsbury, the boys began singing
"Ninety-nine Bottles of Beer on the Wall." The song petered
out at eighty-five bottles. The night before, planning the drive
to Fenway, the boys had closed down the hotel barroom. This
morning they had frequent recourse to the team's water bucket
and dipper.

Jim knew that even Dad drank a cold one at the hotel barroom now and then with his cronies Judge Allen and Doc
Harrison and Prof Chadburn. Maybe what the boys said was
true. Maybe you couldn't become an alcoholic like Hank Williams on beer. Jim himself couldn't claim any credit for not
drinking. He didn't like the taste of beer, or whiskey either,
and he didn't like the way it made him feel. If the other players wanted to drink, that was their business. They were, as
some of them liked to say, "free, white, and twenty-one." Jim
didn't much like the phrase, but so far as it went he supposed it
was true. As long as he was doing the driving, he didn't really
care how much the boys drank.

. . .

"Just Ahead, Second-Longest Covered Bridge in the World."

"Swing in there, Jimbo," Harlan said, pointing at the pull-off beyond the sign. "Pit stop."

Jim nosed the Ark into the pull-off beside a green trash barrel. He got out and stretched. Across the river in New Hampshire the sun was just coming up behind the White Mountains. While the boys went down to pee in the river, Jim read the historical marker beside the entrance of the bridge:

THIS COVERED BRIDGE OVER THE UPPER CONNECT-ICUT RIVER WAS BUILT BY JAMES KINNESON IN 1789. IN 1812, "ABOLITION JIM" RALLIED A CONTINGENT OF LOCAL LOGGERS, TRAPPERS, ABENAKI INDIANS, AND FARMERS AND DECLARED THE INDEPEN-DENCE OF "GOD'S KINGDOM" FROM VERMONT AND THE UNITED STATES OVER THE ISSUE OF SLAVERY. IN 1842, IN A DAYLONG BATTLE AT THIS BRIDGE, JAMES AND EIGHT OF HIS FELLOW SECESSIONISTS WERE KILLED BY FEDERAL SOLDIERS SENT FROM BOSTON TO PUT DOWN THE INSURRECTION, AND KINGDOM COUNTY WAS DULY REINCORPORATED INTO AMERICA.

It seemed strange to Jim to read his own name on the marker. It was almost like reading about his own death.

"I guess old James was pretty independent-minded," Jim said to Charlie.

Charlie laughed. "He was pretty crazy," he said. "Now you know where I get it from."

"Well, looky there, boys," Harlan said, coming back up the bank tugging at his fly. He pointed at an ad painted in white over the arched entryway of the bridge: "Whittemore's Country Store, 1 Mile Ahead in Woodsville, N.H. Coldest Beer in the Granite State."

"They sell beer at Fenway, Harley," Charlie said.

"It's still early in the forenoon, Charlie K. We've got what, seven hours to get there? We'll put her to a vote."

The Knights voted fifteen to two, Charlie and Jim dissenting, to make a beer run to Woodsville. Harlan would direct the Ark across the bridge while Jim drove.

Harlan walked backward into the bridge, holding his arms out at eye level and waggling his fingers for Jim to come ahead. Suddenly there was an incredibly loud crunching noise, followed by the clatter of falling timbers and beams as the entryway of the second-longest covered bridge in the world collapsed onto the roof of the bus.

Jim tried to throw the shifting lever into reverse. Instead he hit first again. His Ked slipped off the clutch and the Ark gave a bound forward. Jim twisted the steering wheel to avoid Harlan. The bus smacked into the north wall of the bridge, knocking some boards down into the river. Finally Jim located reverse. The bus bucked sideways and the black shifting knob came off in his hand. The Ark was wedged diagonally across the bridge with its back wheels and three feet of its rear end hanging out over the river.

Standing in a jackstraw heap of beams and timbers, Harlan nodded. "Yes, sir, gentlemen," he said.

"One thing now," Harlan said as the Knights got out to assess their handiwork. "This ain't young Jim here's fault. Nothing would do but we must make a beer run. I was directing. I checked for width but never looked up. This ain't on Jim's head."

The boys agreed that Jim was in no way responsible for destroying the bridge. Charlie said they should call for a tow truck. He dispatched Cousin Stub Kinneson to a nearby farm on the Vermont side of the river to put in the call. Harlan and the Riendeau brothers volunteered to slope across the river to Whittemore's Country Store and fetch back a case or two of the coldest beer in the Granite State.

Jim walked down the bank and stood beside the river. In the deep pool under the bridge a school of suckers flashed their reddish fins as they scavenged their way along the sandy bottom. Downriver a hundred yards the Boston and Montreal railroad tracks crossed the river on a high trestle. The tow truck would have to arrive soon for the Knights to make batting practice at Fenway.

Harlan and the Riendeaus showed up with eight cases of Black Label in a blue wheelbarrow. Harlan eyed a notice tacked to a soft maple tree near the trash barrel: "Consumption of Alcoholic Beverages Prohibited within 100 Feet of National Monument." Harlan peered inside the trash barrel, then turned it upside down and dumped some sandwich wrappers and empty pop bottles over the bank. He shouldered the barrel, carried it down to the river, and sozzled it out. He brought the barrel back up the bank, got out his church key, and began opening the bottles of Black Label and pouring their contents into the barrel.

"We'll drink turn and turn about out of the water dipper," Harlan explained. "In case anybody comes along."

Cousin Stub returned from the farmhouse to report that the Woodsville wrecker was down for transmission repairs. He'd tried Bradford but couldn't get through. Finally he'd gotten hold of White River. The White River wrecker was out on call but would be up as soon as it got back.

"Hark. I do believe I hear the sound of a si-reen," Harlan said.

Jim heard the siren, too, from across the river. It was coming their way.

A white Ford sedan with blue flashers and "Town of Woodsville Constable" stenciled on the driver's door in red pulled up to the far side of the second-longest covered bridge in the world. A rotund man in a blue uniform and a blue hat with a black chinstrap got out and started across the bridge.

Jim could feel his heart going faster. Maybe the accident wasn't his fault, but he'd been driving at the time.

"What's all this about?" the constable said. "Didn't you fellas see the load limit sign?"

The officer looked into the barrel. "Have you boys been drinking?"

"Certainly not," Harlan said. "We've all tooken the pledge. Our driver, Jim Kinneson here, is sober as a judge."

The policeman surveyed the Knights from under the brim

of his hat. "There's no drinking within one hundred feet of the bridge," he said. "It's a national monument, up on the historical register. I'm afraid I've got to write you boys up."

Traffic was beginning to back up on the Vermont side of the river. The driver of a milk truck with Massachusetts plates laid on his horn, then backed up the hill and turned around in the farmer's barnyard. An older couple from Mississippi stopped to read the historical marker. They stared at the bus trapped on the bridge. "Look at this," the man said to his wife. He pointed at a flyer tacked to the bridge beside the entryway:

Minstrel show, 7 P.M., July 4, Kingdom Common Town Hall. Music, skits, Amos 'n' Andy, Walkin' for de Cake. Admission two dollars, chirren under 12 free.

The woman from Mississippi shook her head. "Vermont," she said to her husband.

Three carloads of PONY League ballplayers on their way from Bradford to a game in North Conway began to chant, "Throw the cop in the river."

"Here, now," the policeman said, putting away his citation book. "You boys want the truth, I'm just a part-time constable, weekends and evenings. Mainly, I'm a Hoover repairman."

The morning was wearing away. There was no word from the towing service in White River. Jim overheard Harlan tell Charlie that Boston might be out the window.

The PONY League team took their lunch down beside the river and had a picnic. Afterward they played flies and grounders in the farmer's cow pasture. Charlie arranged with their

coach for the White Knights of Temperance to play them, the
Knights to bat left-handed. The part-time constable agreed to
umpire from behind the pitcher. By the second inning the
Knights were down 16–0.

In the top of the fourth inning the farmer appeared to report that the first game at Fenway was in the seventh-inning
stretch. The Yankees were ahead 7–2.

"What's the story with White River?" Charlie asked.

"Still out on call," the farmer said. "Their wench cable
snapped in two. They had to send to Barre for a new wench
cable."

Later that inning, a blue hound with a frayed hank of rope
around its neck ran out of the woods onto the playing field.
"Look there, boys," Harlan said. "Somebody's nigger chaser
done got loose."

"Jesus, Harley," Charlie said. Then he looked at Jim. "I
hope you're getting all this down in your head, Mr. Storywriter."

Without quite knowing why, Jim took himself out of the
game and went to sit in the bus, where it was cool and dim and
quiet. After a while he drifted off. When he woke up, it was
late afternoon. The PONY Leaguers had gone home to Bradford. The Sox had lost the first game of the twin bill and were
behind 4–0 in the nightcap.

Some of the boys decided to go skinny-dipping in the pool
under the bridge. A passenger train with a glass-domed ex-
cursion car went by on the trestle and the Knights whooped
and wagged their business at the excursionists. A lady looking
out of the observation car put her hands over her eyes.

The farmer returned to report that there was no further word from White River and the Sox had now fallen behind 8–1 in the second game. The Yankees' ace pitcher, Allie "the Chief" Reynolds, had given up only two scratch hits.

An argument broke out between the Knights over which one of them could "get a bat on one of the Big Injun's fastballs and at least foul it off." Jim believed that he knew the answer to this question but didn't offer his opinion.

Toward evening the Knights held a temperance meeting. They stood around the trash barrel in the pull-off and passed the last dipperful of Black Label from hand to hand. Each team member took a sip and spoke a short piece.

"My name is Stub Kinneson and I believe in a higher power."

"My name is Porter Quinn and I am not an alkie on account of you can't be on beer."

"My name is Faron Wright. I use to be an alkie until I quit the hard stuff."

Faron handed the dipper to Jim, who passed it along to the constable.

"Jim don't drink," Porter explained to the officer. "Not even beer."

"Jim here is living proof that you don't have to drink to have a good time," Stub said.

The constable held up the dipper to toast the White Knights. "From this day onward I am a full-time Hoover repairman," he said. "Here's your tow truck, boys."

The driver from White River wore a cap that read "Junior" over the visor. Junior backed the truck up to the shattered entrance of the bridge. He hitched the tow hook of his new cable to the rear axle of the Ark and winched it back onto the floor of the bridge. A few more timbers and boards rained down into the river.

While the boys negotiated payment, Jim got his jacket out of the bus and walked down to the river one last time. He took the official American League baseball Charlie'd given him out of his jacket pocket and tossed it up in the air and caught it. Then he cocked his throwing arm. Just before Jim hurled the ball as far down the river as he could, Charlie grabbed his wrist. Charlie took the ball from Jim, and on it, with his ballpoint lawyering pen, he printed, "To Jim's girl, Pinky. Love, Joe DiMaggio."

Charlie flipped the ball back to Jim. "Enjoy Montreal, bub. You can borrow my pickup."

To Jim's surprise, the Ark of the Covenant was still drivable after its ordeal, though the steering wheel pulled hard to the right and he had to fight it all the way back to the Common. They arrived at the hotel just as the last strip of light was fading from the sky. The barroom was quiet. Armand was setting the chairs upside down on the tables. The stage behind the chicken wire protecting the band from flying bottles was dark and empty.

"Like thieves in the night," Armand said, handing Jim a Nehi. "The darky run off to Montreal with her fiddler like thieves in the night. I sent the others home for the evening."

Jim got out his signed baseball and set it on the table. He

wished that Charlie had said something more to Harlan about the stray-dog remark. He wished he'd spoken out himself. He supposed he should feel relieved that he hadn't had to watch the Red Sox lose twice in one day to New York, but he didn't. Nor did Pinky ever return to God's Kingdom. For that Jim could scarcely blame her, though for a long time afterward, whenever he thought of her long dark hair and husky voice and the way she'd winked at him, he hoped that she would.

3

The Ballad of Gaëtan Dubois

It must be said that to this day in God's Kingdom, there is a deep and abiding distrust of anyone from "away" or "the other side of the hills."

—PLINY'S *HISTORY*

They appeared in the Kinneson barnyard one afternoon when the air was thick with haze from forest fires across the border in Canada. Jim had been scything off the bank beside the RFD mailbox when he happened to look up and see them. There they were, standing perfectly still, like a family tableau looking silently back at him out of an old-fashioned daguerreotype: an older man and woman, perhaps in their late fifties, dressed in Sunday black, and a tall boy about Jim's age. All three looked slightly apparitional through the haze from the fires, which had been burning out of control in the Laurentian Mountains north of Montreal for several weeks. The boy, too, wore a dark suit, short in the jacket sleeves and trouser legs. Under the jacket he wore a dark shirt buttoned at the collar, and on his feet square-toed brogans that could have been carved from blocks of wood. Between the boy and the old man stood an ox with brass balls on the tips of its horns. No, not an ox. A cow. An ordinary black-and-white milk cow yoked to a wagon piled high with bedsteads and bedding, wooden chairs, a rough table, winter clothing, shovels and pitchforks, a churn and dasher, sap buckets—even an ancient black wood-burning range.

"*Bienvenu, monsieur!*" the old man called out, as if Jim were the stranger. "*Je m'appelle Réjean Dubois. Ma femme, Madame Dubois. Et Gaëtan, notre fils.*"

Madame Dubois nodded politely at Jim. The son, Gaëtan, ducked his head and grinned, as if amused by his talkative father, who was already surveying the Kinneson place with an appraising expression. His quick dark eyes took in the sway-backed hay barn, the overgrown pasture along the river, the empty tenant house across the road.

"*Très belle,*" Réjean said. "You have here, *monsieur, une très belle fermé.* Only she appears to be running away from you a little. I tell you what. I will bring your farm back. I, Réjean Dubois, will make of her a beautiful place."

Réjean clicked to the cow, which bowed its neck into the yoke and plodded across the dirt road and down the lane toward the tenant house. And that is how Gaëtan Dubois and his family came to Kingdom County and took up residence on the Kinneson farm.

Their name, Dubois, meant "of the woods," and out of the woods they had come, the scrubby, cut-over woods and infertile fields full of glacial rocks just north of the Upper Kingdom River marking the border between Vermont and Quebec. "Black French," immigrants from that region were called in the Kingdom of that era. Mixed-blood descendants of the original Abenaki natives, *habitant* French-Canadian farmers, and fugitive slaves from the South who had settled in the area before the Civil War, in the border community known as New Canaan.

"You see, *monsieur?*" Réjean said that evening to Jim's father. "We have come down from the north, us, to make your farm a showplace again."

Jim did not think that the "farm that wasn't," as Gramp sometimes called it, had ever been a showplace. Gramp liked to joke that for generations Kinnesons had used the income from the family newspaper to support the farm and the income from the farm to support the paper. But the editor told Réjean that he and his family were welcome to stay on rent-free at the tenant house for as long as they wished. Jim's mother, Ruth, immediately befriended Madame Dubois.

With Ruth's help, Madame scrubbed the four-room tenant house from top to bottom. From the windows of her new home she hung curtains cut from burlap and dyed red, green, blue, and yellow. Jim helped Réjean and Gaëtan whitewash the milking parlor in the barn. Up went the wood-burning stove in Madame's tiny kitchen. The newcomers were settling in.

Réjean and Gaëtan scythed the wild hay off the disused fields on the hillside behind the farmhouse, raked it into windrows to dry, and pitched it into the wagon for the cow to take to the barn. Réjean got a job on the night shift at the furniture factory in the Common. Madame hired out to clean village houses. Gaëtan helped with chores on neighboring farms. On Sunday afternoons he and Jim went fishing or berrying.

In the long summery evenings after supper, Jim tried to teach his new friend how to play baseball. Flailing away with Jim's thirty-two-inch Adirondack, Gaëtan had no luck making contact with Jim's soft lobs. The Canadian boy knew little English, but one afternoon he repaired the hand-crank starter of Gramp's long-defunct Allis-Chalmers and got it running again. Next he tinkered with the engine of the editor's first car, a Model A Ford blocked up on its rusting wheel rims behind the barn. He attached a belt from the flywheel to a buzz saw and began cutting up firewood for next spring's maple sugaring.

Réjean tapped his head in a canny way and pointed at his son. *"Génie!"* he said to Jim.

Gaëtan shook his head, looked down with his diffident smile. *"Non, Papa,"* he said. *"Albert Einstein est un génie. Moi, non."*

"Oui," Réjean said. "You will see, Monsieur James. When school begins, in the autumn, you will see."

Late each August, Mom and Jim spent an entire day together at the Kingdom Fair. This year they took Gaëtan with them. They started out early in the morning at the animal barns, dropped by the cattle judging, whiled away the heat of the afternoon watching sulky races and the grand cavalcade from the cool of the grandstand. In the early evening they lolly-gagged through the midway, riding all the rides, playing all the games, having a look at Clyde Beatty, the "longest snake in captivity," a sleepy five-foot python in the "Exotic Animals of the World" sideshow. Jim was tremendously proud of his beautiful blond-haired, blue-eyed mother. She went on the Tilt-A-Whirl and dive-bomber with him and Gate, treated them to all the fair food they could hold, and took them to see the Hell Drivers and fireworks highlighting the grandstand show that evening. *"Merci,"* Gaëtan said. *"Merci,* Madame Kinneson. Today has been, how do you say, *un bon temps.* My very good day."

The Kinneson men, including Dad, Gramp, Charlie, and Jim, all had tin ears. Mom loved music. Next to the woodbox in the farmhouse kitchen stood an elderly upright piano, formerly the property of the now-defunct Lost Nation one-room schoolhouse. One Saturday evening Mom invited the Dubois family to join them at the farmhouse for a kitchen junket. Réjean Dubois played the fiddle and clogged his feet to the dozens of Canadian reels he knew by heart. Madame Dubois, a grave, happy expression on her face, accompanied him on a mandolin. Gaëtan clacked two desert spoons together for percussion, and Mom, who'd attended the Boston Conservatory and knew every Beethoven sonata by heart, banged out chords on the hard-used old piano. Charlie and his girlfriend, Athena Allen, stopped by to help eat a washtubful of Gramp's homegrown popcorn, and Madame's French-Canadian *pâtisseries.* At the end of the evening, when Réjean brought them all home with the lilting strains of *"Sucre d'érable,"* even Dad's foot began to tap. Mom looked at Dad's foot, then she looked at Jim and laughed.

Mom was the only person Jim knew who could get away with teasing Dad. She said the reason he couldn't carry a tune was that, except for a few bloody ballads and a handful of Robert Burns's lyrics, music had been outlawed in the Presbyterian Scotland of Dad's ancestors. Come to think of it, Mom said, laughter and fun had been outlawed there, as well. Humor wasn't Dad's strong suit, but Mom could always make him laugh, even at himself. Otherwise, his idea of humor was to say, as he did when he received the Pulitzer Prize, that it and forty cents would buy him a cold one at the Common Hotel. The award committee put out a press release, which Dad refused to run in the *Monitor*. Mom said a Presbyterian Scotsman would rather take up devil worship than take credit for anything. Dad laughed and said it was probably true.

Looking back years later, Jim often thought that Mom's loveliest quality was her rare gift not to wish to please others so much as to be easily pleased herself. Pleased with her gardens, with all kinds of animals, with books and stories, with friends, and most of all, with her family. If Gramp was the chronicler of God's Kingdom, and if Jim's dad, the editor, was its public conscience, Mom was its heart and soul. Gramp put it best. He said it was Mom who introduced joy to the Clan Kinneson.

September arrived. On the first day of school Gaëtan was waiting for Jim at the Kinneson mailbox. He wore the outgrown suit he'd worn on his first day in Vermont and carried a tin lunch pail containing three bread-and-lard sandwiches and a quart canning jar of black coffee. At the Academy, Jim accompanied Gate to the office to help him register. Prof Chadburn, the headmaster, arranged for the boys to take most of their classes together so that Jim could help Gaëtan with his English.

Prof clapped Gate on the shoulder and winked at Jim. "Be sure to sit next to your friend in algebra class," he said. "Let me know if there's any difficulty."

Jim knew that Prof was referring to Miss Hark Kinneson, the longtime math teacher at the Academy and the editor's second cousin once removed. What relation that made her to him Jim neither knew nor cared. Harkness Kinneson was a notorious tyrant who detested all children and young people. Like Prof, she had taught three generations of Commoners. Miss Hark's classes were trials by ordeal and she was universally feared by her students, past and present.

"Welcome to Algebra Two," Miss Hark announced at one o'clock on the Seth Thomas clock over the blackboard of the mathematics room. A rail-thin woman in her late seventies with a mannish jaw, a broad forehead, hands like hay hooks, and small black eyes that missed nothing, Miss Hark surveyed the class bleakly.

"Algebra Two," she continued, "is not metal shop. Algebra Two is not Physical Education. In Algebra Two we will not be playing math games or any games."

Miss Hark delivered these remarks in a flat voice with no hint of humor. In the ensuing silence she reached for a piece of chalk and wrote, on the board, the symbol for pi.

Gaëtan's hand shot up. *"C'est pi, madame le professeur. Trois pointe une quatre une cinq neuf."*

Miss Hark trained her dark little eyes on Gaëtan. "Did I call on you?"

"*Pardon, madame le professeur?*"

"I am neither a madam nor a professor. You will address me as Miss Kinneson. Did I *call on* you?"

"*Oui, Madame.* Pi is, as you say, *un décimal infini. Pardon. Je suis* sad in my *anglais.*"

From the class, a few snickers.

"Silence!" Miss Hark rapped out. She pointed at Gaëtan. "What is your name?"

"Gaëtan," Jim whispered. "*Ton nom?*"

"Oh!" Gaëtan said, grinning. "*Je m'appelle Gaëtan Dubois, madame.*"

"Well, then, Gaëtan Dubois," Miss Hark said. "From this moment onward you will speak only when you are called on and then only in English. Do you understand? English or nothing."

Gaëtan looked back at Miss Hark but said nothing. He said nothing for the rest of the class or the rest of the school day. Gaëtan's definition of pi was the first and last time he spoke in any class at the Kingdom Common Academy until the end of that term. For all he said in school from that day forward, he might as well have been mute.

"Algebra *Deux,*" Gaëtan wrote below his name on his perfect homework assignments. On each of his papers Miss Hark crossed out the word "*Deux*" and wrote beside it "Use English. F." "No scratch work," she'd write in the margin. "Where did you do your scratch work? F."

The standoff continued into October. Gate maintained his silence. Miss Hark did not acknowledge his work or his presence. "I know you are looking on someone else's paper," she wrote on his ungraded midterm exam. "Sooner or later I will prove it." But whose papers was Gaëtan copying? No one else in the class ever got more than a C. Gate never missed a question.

To Jim's amusement, Gaëtan was somewhat superstitious. Sometimes on their way to or from school Gate told him, in his broken English, tales handed down by his *habitant* ancestors north of the border. Jim's favorite was the story of the *loup-garou*, the half-man, half-wolf monster that dwelt in the depths of Lake Memphremagog. The *loup-garou* loved to lure unsuspecting fishermen far out onto the lake on placid summer days, then whip up a sudden tempest and drown them. On moonless nights, and occasionally when the moon was full, the dreaded creature emerged from the lake to roam the forests on both sides of the border, tracking down and devouring lost hunters and disobedient children who'd strayed from home. It was even alleged that the werewolf had deliberately started the Great Forest Fire of 1882.

Gaëtan was uneasy around the skeleton of the Reverend Dr. Pliny Templeton. "Dr. T," as three generations of students had called him, was the founder and first headmaster of the Academy. A former fugitive slave, he'd come north on the Underground Railroad. With the help of his deliverer, later his close friend, Charles Kinneson II, Pliny had put himself through the state university and Princeton Theological Seminary. A renowned minister, educator, abolitionist, and

Civil War hero, Pliny had been shot by his longtime benefactor, Charles, during a dispute over a point of religious doctrine. On those rare occasions when Jim's grandfather and father mentioned the murder, they referred to it only as "the trouble in the family" or, simply, "the trouble."

In his will, Pliny had bequeathed his skeleton to his beloved school as an anatomical exhibit. Although two holes in his skull, front and back, bore eloquent testimony to his murder, and his left hand was missing as well, over the years his skeleton, dangling from a pole at the front of the second-story science lab, had become a kind of mascot to the Academy students, most of whom had grown up in the same building with it since first grade. Not so Gaëtan, who, during his and Jim's late-morning biology class, sat in the back of the room, as far away from the bones as he could get. Jim told his new friend that the state university had proclaimed Pliny Templeton to be the first American Negro college graduate. In honor of the former slave, the university had established a full four-year scholarship in his name, awarded annually to the top-ranking graduate of the Academy. Also, Jim showed Gaëtan Pliny's eleven-hundred-page manuscript in the school library: *The Ecclesiastical, Natural, Social, and Political History of Kingdom County*. No matter. Gaëtan continued to be terrified by the sight of the skeleton, the way Jim felt around snakes and heights. Gate wouldn't even look at the thing, dangling from its pole above the blackboard like a Halloween figure.

Despite the fact that Gate was a mathematical savant, or perhaps partly because of it, Miss Hark continued to bully him at every opportunity. Finally, Jim complained about the math teacher to Mom. Mom's blue eyes snapped and she pursed her lips. That was all, but the next morning she marched into the Academy and closeted herself in the head-master's office with Prof for forty-five minutes.

"He agreed to switch Gaëtan to Mr. Benson's trig class at the end of the term, in January," Mom told Jim that evening. "That's the best I could do, hon."

To Jim, it was obvious that, like nearly everyone else in the Common, Prof was intimidated by Miss Hark Kinneson.

"I'd like to slap her face good and hard," Mom said to Jim. "But of course she'd just take it out on Gate."

"What about forgiving her because she knows not what she does?" Jim kidded her.

"She knows very well what she's doing," Mom said. "We'll leave it to Jesus to forgive her, sweetie. That's more than I can muster right now."

"Do you believe in Jesus, Mom?"

"I believe in love," Mom said. "And, I'm afraid, in its absence."

In early November, Réjean bought two more milking cows. With some of the earnings from her housekeeping jobs, Madame Dubois purchased a Toulouse laying goose. Once or twice a week Gaëtan brought a hard-boiled goose egg to school to eat with his lard sandwiches and coffee.

With Thanksgiving week came the onset of winter in the Kingdom. As usual, the volunteer fire department flooded the ball diamond on the village green and set up sideboards for a hockey rink. Gaëtan appeared on the ice with a pair of hand-me-down skates and a homemade hockey stick. Once again Jim learned something surprising about his friend. The gangling kid who couldn't connect with a baseball skated like the north wind out of Canada. In the first five minutes of their first pickup game, Gaëtan made a hat trick. He spent the rest of the game drawing out the goalie, then dropping off the puck to teammates for open shots on the net.

On skates, Gaëtan Out-of-the-Woods was indomitable. In brushups with players from neighboring towns who called him a "Black Canuck," and worse, he'd windmill his arms and fists without much strategy, but no matter how hard you hit him you couldn't knock him down. At some point he'd get his licks in and then you'd be sorry you'd taunted him.

On New Year's Day, when gifts were traditionally exchanged in French Canada, Réjean and Madame presented Gaëtan with a new pair of hockey skates. He and Jim skated up the frozen Lower Kingdom River to the colony of multicolored ice-fishing shanties on the South Bay of Lake Memphremagog. Gaëtan pointed north up the lake between the mountains across the border. "*Chez soi,*" he said. Home.

On the morning of Miss Hark's algebra final, the mercury in the Kinnesons' outdoor thermometer sat at twenty-seven below zero. The air sparkled with ice crystals from the mist over the High Falls in the village. Walking the half mile into town, their skates laced together and slung over their shoulders, Jim and Gaëtan were half frozen by the time they reached the Academy.

There was no way to keep the big granite school warm in weather that cold. Even the basement room, with its monstrous coal-burning furnace, was frigid. Most students took their tests in their winter coats and boots. At lunch, Gaëtan's coffee steamed like a boiling kettle.

Miss Hark's Algebra II test was scheduled from one to three. Mr. Benson's juniors were taking their trig exam in the math room that period, so the algebra test was moved to the science lab. As Jim walked into the room, he felt his breathing tighten at the sight of the exams stacked on the corner of the teacher's desk. The scent of fresh mimeograph ink hung on the air like ether in an operating room. From its pole at the front of the room, Pliny Templeton's skeleton seemed to be grinning out at the students, delighted by their apprehensive expressions. As usual, Gaëtan sat in the back of the room.

At precisely one o'clock, Miss Hark marched up and down the aisles passing out the test papers. With a sinking heart, Jim riffled through the exam. There was an entire page of word problems that might have given Einstein himself pause. The first one began, "A runaway locomotive traveling at 96 mph is hurtling down upon the Academy team bus, stalled on the crossing in Kingdom Common, 3.4 miles away, with the bus door and emergency exit frozen shut." Across the aisle to Jim's left a single tear slid down Becky Sanville's cheek, whether for her own plight or for that of the doomed students on the bus was impossible to know.

At one fifteen, Gaëtan stood up, walked to the front of the

room, and placed his completed test on Miss Hark's desk. Jim noticed that he approached the desk on the far side from Pliny's skeleton.

"What?" she said.

For the first time in four months, Gaëtan spoke in school. "J'ai finis," he said.

"Speak English. This is America."

Miss Hark picked up Gate's test and glanced at it. "There's only one way you could possibly be finished, Dubois. You got your hands on a copy of the examination ahead of time. Where did you get it? Out of the teachers' room?"

Gaëtan shook his head. "No, madame. Mademoiselle."

Miss Hark stood up. "Then where is your scratch work? Show me."

Gaëtan shrugged, then touched his head to indicate that was where he did his figuring. At the same time, he glanced at the skeleton.

"What are you looking at?" Miss Hark said. "Why are you looking at me that way? Are you mocking me?"

"I don't look you. I look him. I don't like."

"Oh, you don't, don't you? Well, how do you like this?"

Very deliberately, Miss Hark tore Gaëtan's exam in two and dropped it into the wastebasket beside her desk. She stood up, turned to the blackboard, and drew a small circle just above the chalk tray, at about waist height, inches from the dangling skeleton. "Bend over, Monsieur Dubois," she said. "Nose in the circle."

Jim jumped to his feet, so angry he was shaking. "He didn't cheat, Miss Hark. I'll go in his place."

"You'll do no such thing, Kinneson. Sit down this instant. Get back to work. All of you, get back to work."

Gaëtan, already bent over at the blackboard with his nose in the circle, motioned for Jim to sit down. As terrified as he was of the bones, this was between him and Miss Hark.

"You may resume your seat, Dubois," Miss Hark said, "when, and only when, you confess to cheating."

As the afternoon wore on, clouds began to sail in from the northwest. The wind picked up and the classroom windows rattled in their wooden sashes. Stooped over at the blackboard, Gaëtan reached under his tattered jacket and rubbed the small of his back. From time to time he twisted his head and glanced fearfully at the skeleton. Jim thought about going for Prof but didn't. Gaëtan seemed determined to fight this battle himself.

At two twenty-five Gaëtan waved his hand. "Mademoiselle Kin'son," he said. "*S'il vous plaît.*"

"Are you ready to confess, Dubois?"

"*Je dois aller aux toilettes, Mademoiselle.*"

"Fine. When you admit that you cheated on your examination, you may go to the boys' room. Not until."

Gaëtan lifted one large brogan, then the other, like a nervous horse. Jim thought of the quart jar of coffee his friend had drunk at lunch. The boy must be in agony.

Across the aisle, Becky gasped. Her hand shot to her mouth. She was staring at Gate, bent over in his too-small suit like a ragged old man. The entire class was staring at Gaëtan. A stream of liquid came pouring out of the frayed cuffs of his trousers, splashing over his square-cut shoes onto the floor of the classroom. On and on it came, more than Jim would have thought possible.

Miss Hark frowned at the class. She looked over her shoulder at the clock. "You still have five minutes. Double-check your—"

Miss Hark made a strangled noise in her throat and lurched to her feet. She pointed at Gaëtan, standing in the spreading pool of his own urine, then at the door. "Go!" she shrieked. "Get out."

Gaëtan remained bent over at the blackboard. "I do not cheat, me!" he shouted.

"I don't care if you cheated or not. Get out of my class, you stinking Black Frenchman."

Gaëtan shook his head. "With respect, Mademoiselle. I do not cheat."

The puddle at Gaëtan's feet crept toward Miss Hark's desk. She started to back away. Just as she bolted for the door, it opened and Prof stepped into the room. "Excuse me, Miss Hark. The hockey game this afternoon's been canceled because of the weather. There's a major blizzard coming in from Canada. I want you boys and girls to bundle up and go straight—Miss Hark? Are you all right?"

"Him!" Miss Hark shrieked, pointing at Gaëtan. Then she rushed past Prof and out the door.

At the blackboard, Gaëtan straightened up and turned to face the class. A dark stain covered the front of his trousers.

"*Pardon,*" Gaëtan said. "*Pardon, monsieur le professeur. J'ai* shame."

Eyes down, Gaëtan walked to the back of the classroom and removed his overcoat from its hook. He threw his new skates over his shoulder, picked up his lunch pail, and left the room.

"This is most unfortunate," Prof told the class. "I'm sorry you folks had to witness something like this."

"Prof," Jim said. "Miss Hark accused Gate of cheating, but he didn't."

"I know he didn't, son," Prof said. "You go find your friend and tell him I know he didn't do anything wrong. The rest of you people are dismissed. Leave your tests on your desks. I'll collect them."

As the students got to their feet, Prof said, "Keep your faces covered up on your way home. It's murderously cold out there."

Gaëtan's brogans sat side by side on the riverbank. On the dark ice below, Jim made out the diagonal telemarks of Gaëtan's long skating strides. Hurriedly he kicked off his boots and laced up his skates. Jim knew that he could never overtake his friend in an all-out race. He had to hope that Gate would stop to thaw out at one of the fishing shanties on the South Bay.

As Jim skated north up the river, tracing its oxbows through the frozen wetlands south of the lake, the wind buffeted his body like a hockey defenseman checking him at every turn. He had to twist his head aside to breathe. He tried burying his mouth and nose in the fleece collar of his jacket, but when he did, his breath froze to his face. He covered the five miles through the swamp to the bay in thirty minutes. Gaëtan's skate tracks, silvery in the dwindling light of the short winter afternoon, continued past the enclave of fishing shacks toward the big lake and Canada.

The wind funneling through the notch between the mountains struck Jim with frightening force. The peaks of Kingdom and Canada Mountains were obscured by blowing snow. Far to the southwest the sun was a pewter disc. It touched the peak of Mt. Mansfield, then vanished.

Something came hurtling Jim's way, tumbling wildly across the ice. As it rattled past him, he recognized Gaëtan's lunch pail. Jim thought of Gate's wet trousers and socks, frozen stiff by now.

Briefly the gale let up, as if gathering itself for a more fierce assault. Just ahead, at the Great Earthen Dam, the Upper Kingdom River marking the Canadian border flowed into the lake from the east. Suddenly Jim knew where Gaëtan was headed. He was going home.

North of the dam, the lake rarely froze until mid-January. In the last blue light of the day, Jim could see whitecaps angling from shore to shore. He heard the breakers crashing. He was almost out of ice.

Jim skidded sideways, stumbled, regained his balance, and came to a stop. The wind picked up again, and he had to lean into it to stay on his feet as he screamed out Gaëtan's name again and again. He thought of his friend standing at the blackboard in a pool of his own urine. He thought of himself doing nothing to help Gate, even when Miss Hark had called him a "Black Frenchman," and of Prof's last words to the class.

"It's murderously cold out there," Prof had told them, and it was. Yet somehow Jim knew, as he started back down the ice with the howling wind at his back, that however treacherous the cold and snow and wind and fathomless dark heart of the lake might be, the greater dangers of this place they called God's Kingdom lay closer to home.

4

Haunted

In those years every village in the Kingdom boasted its own haunted house.

—PLINY'S *HISTORY*

It was May Day in Kingdom County. This was the time of year when Jim and his close friend and fishing mentor, Prof Chadburn, would toss their fly rods in the back of Prof's Rambler station wagon and head out the county road along the river to fish the rainbow run. They'd spend the entire day on the stream, stopping at noon to cook their catch over an open fire for a shore lunch, fishing on through the afternoon together for the gigantic silver-and-crimson trout that ran up the river to spawn in the spring of the year.

Not today. Today Prof had recruited his prize Latin student and star shortstop on the Academy baseball team to help him empty out Miss Hark Kinneson's former house in the village. This was Saturday. The past Monday, before the students arrived at the Academy, Prof had stepped discreetly into Miss Hark's classroom to tell her that her employment would be terminated with the end of the current school year. He'd discovered the math teacher slumped over with her head on her desk, her eyes wide open and glaring angrily out over what had been her domain for fifty years, as if she'd divined his intention and upstaged him. To his further astonishment, a few days later Prof learned that he had inherited Miss Hark's house, just across the street from the north end of the village green.

Prof may well have been the only Commoner to whom the news that Harkness Kinneson had named him her heir came unexpectedly. The whole town, including Jim, knew that Miss Hark had set her cap for John Chadburn from the day they entered high school together. Unfortunately for the future schoolmistress, by then young Johnny was already in love with the remote trout streams and deep woods of the Kingdom.

Over his long tenure as headmaster at the Academy, Prof had become something of a living legend in God's Kingdom. A burly man with thinning white hair, a neat gray mustache, and noticing blue eyes, he still taught four classes of Latin and coached Jim's baseball team. Malefactors actually enjoyed being sent to his office. After roaring at them for a minute or two, he regaled them with tales of his own juvenile misdemeanors, then sent them back to class laughing. To cover up his bald spot he wore his Academy baseball cap indoors and out, year-round.

As the old Rambler rattled onto the one-lane red iron bridge over the river, Prof slowed to a crawl. He looked out his window and Jim looked out his at the river below. Jim thought he saw the dark outline of a trout shoot up through the current into the shadow of the bridge abutment. Hanging in the deep green bridge pool, the fish looked nearly as long as Jim's arm.

"Well, son," Prof said as they continued into the village, "I don't need to tell you how little I look forward to this business today. Or how much I appreciate your help."

Jim nodded. But as they pulled up to the curb in front of Miss Hark's place, he was quite sure that Prof didn't dread the day ahead as much as he did. Not only had the recently deceased math teacher been directly responsible for the terrible fate of his friend Gaëtan Dubois on the big lake, her village house was widely rumored to be haunted. Never once in his nearly sixteen years had Jim set foot inside the place, and as foolish as he knew this was, he'd fervently hoped never to have to.

The old Kinneson manse, as Miss Hark's place was called, had been built by Jim's great-great-grandfather "Abolition Jim" Kinneson. Abolition Jim had constructed the manse for his wife, who was unhappy on the farm where Jim and his parents now lived and pined for a place in town. Although not as large or stately as Judge Allen's home on Anderson Hill, or Prof's headmaster's house, the manse had several handsome features. Old James had cut a sideways, or "coffin," window between the steep upper slate roof and the tin roof of the kitchen ell. Into the front wall of the second story, overlooking the village green to the south, James had built an elegant secluded porch. A flagstone walk led from the picket fence up to

the front door, over which he had inserted a horizontal transom of six frosted panes. A set of sleigh bells hung beside the
door. Callers at the manse announced their arrival by giving
them a shake. In the old days, visitors would sometimes jingle
the bells a second time for the sheer pleasure of hearing them
again. Atop the carriage shed adjacent to the house was a copper weathervane in the shape of a galloping Morgan horse. A
bed of lavender scented the narrow side lawn between the
manse and the lane leading down to the High Falls on the river.
A few tiny white violets grew between the flagstones.

Just when the manse was first proclaimed to be haunted
was lost in the distant lore of the village. Nor was Jim sure
who or what was supposed to possess the place. Children, always more keenly attuned to these matters than their elders,
began crossing the street to the village green in order to avoid
walking by the manse about the time Miss Hark inherited the
house from James's widow, her Kinneson grandmother.

Over the decades the place had fallen into disrepair. Virginia creeper had twined up the outside walls. A few of the
square nails holding the roof slates in place had rusted out.
Several slates had pulled free and fallen onto the lawn below
or shattered on the flagstone walk. The copper horse on the
carriage shed had acquired a sickly verdigris patina, as if it had
become nauseated from its own air of perpetual motion.

It was said that the manse contained a secret chamber,
where Miss Hark's father had hidden fugitive slaves before
smuggling them across the border to Canada. Some Commoners swore that they'd heard snatches of old spirituals

coming from the front parlor late at night, accompanied by the wheezing strains of the ancient pump organ that had belonged to James's widow.

While Prof sorted through a ring of iron keys, Jim tugged on the sleigh bells. Prof gave a start. "Jesum Crow!" he said.

Jim struggled not to laugh out loud. Evidently Prof was as frightened of the manse as he was. The vestibule and front hallway smelled cold and stale, like a disused church. A curved staircase led to the second story. Prof laid his hand on one of the carved balusters. "Butternut," he said. "You don't see much butternut being used in houses these days, Jimmy. This house was *built*."

He poked his head into the front parlor off the hall. "And just look at this wainscoting. Bird's-eye maple all the way up to the chair rail. I played here with Harkness as a kid. I never would have noticed how pretty the woodwork was then."

"Are you going to move in?"

"I'll have to have someplace to hang my fish pole after I retire," Prof said. "The headmaster's house goes with the job."

"I wouldn't live in a haunted house for a million dollars," Jim said.

Prof grinned. He touched one bushy eyebrow, then his lips, then made a circle of his thumb and forefinger: their private code for "I say nothing."

"Truth to tell," Prof said, "I've never thought it was the house that was haunted."

There wasn't much to see in the parlor. A horsehair love seat with yellowed antimacassars on its arms and back. Two

uncomfortable-looking Morris chairs. The antiquated organ rumored to play itself. A glass-fronted bookcase containing old-fashioned romance novels from the era of Jim's
grandparents and great-grandparents. "I don't think this room
has been used since the manse was a boardinghouse, Jim,"
Prof said.

"I didn't know it ever was a boardinghouse."

"Oh, yes, and within my memory. After Abolition Jim was
killed by federal troops and the Kingdom was reincorporated
into the nation, James's widow operated a very respectable
boardinghouse here, mainly for traveling single ladies and
old-maid schoolteachers and such. She willed the place to her
grown granddaughter Harkness—speaking of old-maid
schoolteachers. Miss H continued to run the boardinghouse
for a few years after she inherited it. Then she got her normal-
school degree and started working at the Academy. That's
about when the boarding business went by the board. Sorry
for the bad pun."

They returned to the hallway, which led into a dining room.
A trestle-style table with twelve ladder-back chairs arranged
around it took up most of the space in the room.

Out in the ell, the pale-yellow kitchen linoleum gleamed
from a recent waxing. Next to the deep-welled zinc sink sat an
icebox, as Prof referred to it, with a squat round motor on top.
It was unplugged and the door was ajar. Except for an open
box of baking soda, the shelves were bare. A massive black
Home Comfort cooking and heating stove, converted at some
point from wood to gas, sat between the empty icebox and the
door to the woodshed. Off the kitchen was a narrow bath-

room, formerly a pantry, Prof thought, containing a toilet with a pull-chain attached to an overhead water tank, and a tub with high sides resting on lion-claw feet.

Another door led from the kitchen to a downstairs bedroom. Prof told Jim that he believed that Miss Hark had slept here for decades. Her severe dark teaching dresses hung in a wooden chifforobe. An oak dresser contained clean, folded blouses, sweaters, and underthings. Beside Miss Hark's narrow brass bed was a stack of books on a washstand. Prof read the titles out loud to Jim. *Jane Eyre, Wuthering Heights, Pride and Prejudice.* He shook his head, touched one eyebrow, then his lips, and shot Jim the thumb-and-forefinger sign.

Upstairs in the master bedroom off the secluded porch, Prof and Jim discovered several dozen cardboard boxes filled with graded examinations dating all the way back to Miss Hark's first years as a math teacher at the Academy. "Look at this, Prof!" Jim said, holding up a blue test booklet. " 'Charles Kinneson III. November 4, 1915. Algebra II. D -. Did not follow assignment.' "

Charles III was Jim's father, the Pulitzer Prize–winning editor of *The Kingdom County Monitor,* whose scathing columns on Senator Joseph McCarthy had helped lead to McCarthy's recent censure on the floor of the Senate. It was as if Miss Hark, otherwise not a hoarder, had held on to the exam papers all these years to maintain power over her now-grown former students.

"These boxes and what's in them need to go to the dump,"

Prof said. "I'll lug them down to the front door and you put 'em in the back of the Rambler." This time Prof didn't bother to flash Jim the "I say nothing" signal. He was angered, and unsettled as well, by the discovery of the exams.

For the rest of the morning Jim loaded boxes into Prof's station wagon and ran them up to the village dump on the back side of Anderson Hill. Crazy Kinneson, Jim's second cousin, helped him heave the old examinations onto the smoky fire of discarded treadless tires, broken boards, and household garbage that smoldered day and night at the dump in those days. An unstoppable center on the Academy basketball team, Crazy lived with his uncle the dumpkeeper in a shack constructed of old lumber and packing crates. For company he conversed with an array of imaginary companions, both living and dead.

"Tell Miss Hark that Crazy says hello, Jimmy," Crazy said. "Tell the pretty dark lady hello, too."

Jim liked Crazy and was accustomed to his strange pronouncements. Privately, he thought that his cousin might not be crazy at all. Jim waved to Crazy out the window of the Rambler and headed back toward the manse.

At noon Prof sprang for Armand St. Onge's famous hot roast pork sandwiches at the hotel dining room. The dining room was crowded this noon, with both local and out-of-state fishermen. Jim's brother, Charlie, and Charlie's girlfriend, Athena Allen, Jim's much-beloved English teacher at the Academy,

waved Prof and Jim over to a table by the window, overlooking the railroad crossing at the north end of the village green.
"How are you guys coming over at Miss Havisham's?" Charlie said. "Did you bring us a slice of her wedding cake?"

Athena gave Charlie a look. "Speaking of weddings," she
said.

Jim grinned. He was a little shy around his favorite teacher
because she was so beautiful. He didn't understand why his
big brother didn't marry her and neither, Charlie'd recently
confided to him, did he. Jim surely would have. In Charlie's
place he'd have married his good-looking teacher long ago. Jim
would have given anything to have a whip-smart, funny,
Hollywood-gorgeous girlfriend like Athena Allen, who encouraged him with his storywriting and never wrote "Did not
follow assignment" on his compositions—though he often did
not—at the same time that she teased him, fondly and mercilessly, like a big sister, calling him a "daydreaming romantic,"
often adding that she wished "you know who" was a little more
like him. Privately, Jim worried that Charlie would let
Athena slip through his fingers.

Charlie and Athena had been on the river since dawn and
were still wearing their waders. As usual, they were arguing.
In fact, Jim could not remember a time when Charlie and his
longtime girlfriend had not been arguing. Mom said that arguing was how Charlie and Athena conversed with each
other, which Jim supposed was the case, though he wished
that when they were conversing, they wouldn't try to enlist
him on behalf of their respective causes.

Today the couple was engaged in a debate over the size of a trout Athena had lost in the basin pool below the High Falls behind the hotel. She'd played it for several minutes, and it had jumped twice, so both Charlie and Athena had gotten a good look at it. But when Charlie had tried to net it for her, he'd inadvertently—or not—knocked it off the hook. Athena claimed the fish weighed at least six pounds. Charlie said four pounds was more like it.

"Your so-called teacher here, Jimmy, is accusing me of deliberately causing her to lose that mediocre trout," Charlie said. "Would I do that?"

Outside, the long noon freight was rumbling by. Charlie had to speak just below a shout to make himself heard. So did Athena when she said, "What do you mean 'so-called teacher'? I *am* Jim's teacher. Your brother bumped that fish off my hook on purpose, Jim. All he caught all morning was a pathetic little fingerling and he was jealous. It's the sort of thing I'd have expected him to do when we were twelve."

Jim gave Prof a pleading look, hoping he'd intervene and get him down from the witness stand. The old headmaster, however, was watching the train go by and only half paying attention to the conversation. Like many men who'd grown up in the Common during its heyday as a railroad town, with a roundhouse where mechanics worked on hundred-ton steam engines, and thirty trains a day passing through the village, Prof loved everything about railroading. When Prof was a boy, and for decades afterward, the railroad was the town's main link to away, the other side of the hills. It was how Commoners got to St. Johnsbury to shop and to the matinees in Memphremagog. Jim loved trains, too, especially the exotic-sounding names on the sides of the freight cars. Baltimore and Ohio. Pine Tree State. Great Northern. Grand Trunk. Jim loved the names of the railroad lines the way he loved the names of Gramp's hand-tied trout flies and Mom's old-fashioned apple trees on the farm that wasn't.

At last, the caboose rattled over the crossing. A mile away, at the trestle north of town, one of the four diesel engines whistled. As the whistle faded away, a brief lull settled over the hotel dining room and the village, an empty quietude that Jim always found slightly melancholy.

"I'll net my own fish from now on, buster," Athena said to Charlie. "Wouldn't you, Jimmy?"

This time Prof came to his rescue. He pointed his crooked index finger, broken twice from his glory days as a standout catcher at the Academy, at the squabbling couple. "Enough," he said. "I listened to your catfights for four years when you two were going to school. I don't intend to have my dinner ruined by them today. Charlie, what's the farthest you've ever seen a baseball hit on the common?"

Charlie looked out the dining room window, across the railroad tracks at the bandstand, and on down the green toward the baseball backstop at the far south end. "A few years ago my cousin Moose Kinneson tagged one off the upper story of the brick shopping block across the street from deep left field. There's no telling how far it might have traveled. Four hundred and fifty feet? Maybe five hundred."

Prof nodded. "I remember that. I was umping behind the plate that day. But that wasn't the longest ball I ever saw hit here. The longest ball was one I hit, by sheer blind luck, when I was just out of the service and playing town ball. We were facing a fireball pitcher, one of those crazy Carter boys out of the Landing, and I literally closed my eyes and 'swang from the heels,' as old John McGraw used to say. Somehow, I connected. I lambasted that old grass-stained baseball clear over the bandstand in center field.

"Well, the Montreal Flyer—a misnomer if there ever were one—just happened to be passing through town at the time. I thought the ball I hit was going to clear the train, maybe bounce off the steps of the hotel porch. Instead, a fella in a seersucker suit and a blue-and-white boater hat, smoking a cigar on the rear platform of the caboose, reached up and caught that baseball one-handed, neat as you please. He made as if to throw it back onto the green but instead he dropped the ball in his jacket pocket. Then he lifted his hat in our direction and made a little bow, and he was still bowing and tipping that foolish boater hat as the caboose passed out of sight. A howl went up from both teams. That was our only ball, you see. Stealing our baseball was about the meanest thing we'd ever seen a man do."

"You didn't see this one lose my trophy fish for me," Athena said, nodding at Charlie.

Charlie laughed, but Prof, still looking out the window as if at the man in the seersucker suit making off with the team's only baseball, said, "We scrounged up another ball from somewhere or other and finished the game. I'm pretty sure we lost, but at least we were left with something to talk about. And with a grievance, too, which of course was almost as satisfying as a win over a much-despised rival. One day a month or so later a package arrived at the post office. It was about the size of a shoebox, and addressed to the "Baseball Players, General Delivery, Kingdom Common, Vermont." That's all. No return address. Old Cap Wally Bowen, our playing manager, opened it up and inside were two baseballs. No note or other explanation. Just the balls. One was grass-stained and scuffed, like the one I'd whacked over the bandstand. The other was brand-new, white as fresh paint, with bright-red stitching and that wonderful horsehide scent that of all the things in the world only a baseball has. What's more, that new baseball had been signed. It was signed by Ty Cobb and every other member of the 1906 Detroit Tigers. And under Cobb's signature, in the same flourishing handwriting, it said, 'Back to you, fellas.'"

"Wow!" Athena said.

"Great story," Charlie said. But Prof wasn't finished.

"My point," he said, "is that in the realm of human affairs, people aren't always exactly who they seem to be. Look, it was said that Cobb would spike his own grandma, if necessary, to steal second base. I'm sure he would have. But there was more to him than that. And that's the point."

"What happened to the baseballs?" Jim said.

Prof gave him an approving look. "That's just the kind of question I'd expect a storywriter to ask. What happened is I put them on top of that glass-fronted bookcase in my office at the Academy and a year or so later the damn things vanished without a trace. At first I was mad, but after I cooled down, I figured some kid was getting the good out of them in a cow pasture or vacant lot, and that's what a baseball was meant for. This meal's on me, kiddos."

Prof stood up and tipped his cap to Athena. "Ma'am," he said. Then he shook Charlie's hand.

To Jim he said, "Let's hit the high dusty, son. No rest for the wicked."

Before returning to Miss Hark's place, Jim and Prof walked down the lane through the field behind the manse to watch the rainbow trout jumping the High Falls on their way upriver to spawn. The run was at its peak this weekend. Several fish a minute fought their way up through the rapids, arcing out of the water to clear the falls, their crimson sides flashing in the spring sunshine. Jim inhaled the fresh scent of the aerated water. He was dying to feel the pulsing weight of a fish on the end of his line. Prof clapped him on the shoulder. "I know, son," he shouted over the roar of the cataract below. "You feel like the detained wedding guest in the poem. Don't give up hope. We may yet sneak in an hour on the bridge pool before nightfall."

Jim had no idea who the detained wedding guest was or what poem Prof was referring to, but how many warm Saturdays in early May when the rainbow run was on did a young fisherman have in his life?

An impossibly red male trout Jim estimated would weigh between seven and eight pounds leaped, hit the lip of the flume, and was knocked back down the current. It gathered itself in the holding pool below the falls, then shot up the cataract again.

This time it tailwalked the last foot or two over the top of the falls into the calmer water above.

"How do they do it, Prof? It's like they defy gravity."

"It's their matrimonial instinct, son. That's the strongest force there is. Stronger than gravity, even. You'll know when the time comes."

Another huge trout cartwheeled its way up and over the thundering waterfall. Prof grinned. "I felt like that once."

Suspecting that a story was about to follow, Jim waited silently. Already, he was beginning to learn that the fewer questions he asked, the more people were apt to tell him. Especially in the Kingdom, no one liked too many questions.

Prof retreated several steps back from the edge of the bank, where they could speak without shouting. "It was the late summer of '99. I'd been home from that hoo-ha in Cuba for a month or two. I'd just hired on to teach Latin and ancient history at the Academy. Somehow, I'd also managed to get myself appointed justice of the peace for Kingdom Common. The old justice, Judge Benson, was ailing, and nobody else wanted the job so the town fathers hung it on me.

"One evening a few days before the school term started, Ephraim Fairbrother, the town constable, showed up at my place with a young woman in tow. A very attractive young woman, I might add. She had dark eyes and hair and a dark complexion, like one or two Cuban gals I'd gotten to know down below, and a figure like—oh my, Jim, she had a figure. I couldn't tell for sure, but I wouldn't have guessed she was a day over twenty. Well, Old Man Fairbrother, who didn't have the sense God gave a gnat, had hauled her up in front of me for peddling without a license, and for vagrancy. But as the girl was quick to point out, she wasn't a peddler at all. She was a traveling dressmaker from Montreal. She'd breeze into a town, take a room at a boardinghouse or hotel, and make arrangements to model her dresses for the better-off ladies of the area. She had a dress for every occasion. Being such a beauty herself, she'd have looked good in a washerwoman's smock, much less an expertly tailored evening gown, so of course she always got a good number of orders for bespoke dresses. For a modest down payment, she'd take a lady's measurements, and when she'd accumulated enough orders, she'd go back to Montreal and make them tailored dresses.

"Well, Jimmy. That comely young seamstress was as mad as a blue-tailed hornet. She said she was no more a common peddler than 'the old gendarme' was the 'bishop of Montreal.' As for being a vagrant, she was boarding at the manse, and she assured me that Miss Hark would most certainly give her a good name. She said that if I wished to verify her claims, I could come over to the manse and she'd model her dresses in a private show just for me.

"Needless to say, son, I swallowed the bait. The very next evening I took her to dinner at the hotel. The following night I squired her to a dance at the town hall. She wore a short, flouncy red dress with matching open-toed heels. Jim, every man at that dance was jealous of me and every woman hated her. And dance? Why, she floated over the floor as if she'd been dancing as long as she'd been walking. Those dark eyes of hers were shy and bold at the same time, and she had what you'd call a fetching accent. Not French. Maybe Eastern European. Actually, I think she was part gypsy."

"What was her name?"

"Sophia. Her name was Sophia. I called her Sophie. That night when I took her back to the manse she let me kiss her and mister man, you can just imagine. We made a date to go buggy riding the next afternoon, but when I showed up at the manse with a hired trap from the livery stable—she was gone."

"Gone!" Jim said. Then, despite his resolution not to interrupt, "Gone where?"

"Miss Hark said an urgent telegram had come from Montreal very early that morning. It was bad news. Sophie's sister had died. Sophie'd left in her black funeral dress, the same one she'd modeled for her customers, and a black veil, on the dawn Flyer. And that was the last I ever heard of her."

"She never came back? Or wrote?"

"Nope. I went up to Montreal to look for her and pounded the sidewalks of the garment district, but a gypsy, you know, can vanish into thin air in a room with just two people in it, much less a great city."

Prof stared at the rushing river. Finally he shrugged. "It couldn't ever have come to anything, whatever there was between us. Other than the fact that we were both young, we didn't have a thing in common. I was a village schoolteacher. She was as wild and free as—" Prof flipped the back of his hand toward the falls—"one of those leaping trout."

There was so much more that Jim wanted to know, but all

Prof said, as they cut back across the field toward the manse, was, "You'll have to write the story yourself someday, son."

"How?" Jim said. "I don't know the ending."

"That's all right," Prof said. "Leave it a mystery, then."

Jim finished his last dump run late that afternoon. It looked as though he and Prof might get their fishing in after all, but first Prof wanted to "take a gander" at the carriage shed. Jim slyly asked him what he proposed to do in the shed with a male goose and Prof snatched off his Academy ball cap and made as if to flail his student about the head and shoulders with it. Two good friends and fishing chums, horsing around after a fraught day.

They didn't find much in the shed. A one-horse run-around pung, a larger cutter on ornately curved runners that had belonged to Miss Hark's father. A grain bin next to the door leading to a two-stall stable.

Jim lifted the heavy lid of the bin and peered inside. Empty. "Maybe this is where the runaway slaves hid," he said.

Prof chuckled. "I'd forgotten all about the so-called secret slave chamber. Come on back to the house, Jim. I'll show you. Then we'll hit the bridge pool."

In the front hallway of the manse, Prof showed Jim a china knob, not much larger than a shooter aggie, in the paneling below the curving staircase. It opened outward, revealing a small space under the stairs. "Harkness and I used to play hide-and-seek in there," Prof said. "Rumor had it that's where the fugitive slaves were hidden, but I've always been skeptical.

There was a saying that here in the Kingdom, the Underground Railroad ran aboveground. Slavecatchers didn't dare venture up to these parts. If they did, they never went back. Crawl in there, Jim. See if there's anything worth looking at."

In the back of the cubbyhole beneath the stairs, under a throw rug, Jim discovered a trunk. "Geehaw it out," Prof said. "Maybe that's where Miss H kept her nest egg. If so, I'll split it with you, fifty-fifty."

The trunk was wedged under the exposed underside of the staircase. By degrees Jim worked it over to the door. Together, he and Prof wrestled it through the opening into the hallway. Jim crawled out after the trunk and took a deep breath, glad to be out of the cubbyhole.

"Or," Prof said, "it could contain some old slavecatcher's bones. Be my guest, Jim. Open it up."

"I'll leave that honor to you, Prof."

The slanted rays of the lowering sun, dancing with motes, fell through the frosted glass transom above the front door onto the old chest. As Prof clicked open the hasp and lifted the lid, the sunlit hallway was suffused with the scent of lavender. Desiccated lavender blossoms, as blue as Prof's eyes, lay inside on several large albums. Brushing aside the still-fragrant flowers, Prof lifted out one of the volumes and began to leaf through the brittle pages. It was a scrapbook containing clippings about Prof from the *Monitor*, some with photographs. Prof at about Jim's age, in his baggy baseball uniform, wearing a catcher's mitt. Prof in a graduation cap and gown, delivering his valedictory address. And a few years later, in puttees and a uniform blouse with lieutenant's stripes, standing in front of a military tent with a young Teddy Roosevelt. Other scrapbooks in the lavender-scented trunk contained articles on championship Academy teams Prof had coached and trophy trout he'd landed, and Prof's entire speech upon receiving the Vermont Headmaster of the Year award. And then, two baseballs, one scuffed and grass-stained, the other signed with the just-discernible names of the 1906 Detroit Tigers. Jim couldn't help laughing, but Prof was visibly nonplussed.

"My goodness, Jimmy," he said. "I don't know whether this is a shrine or a mausoleum or both. Let's keep this between ourselves, shall we?"

Below the scrapbooks were some toilet articles. A hand mirror backed in mother-of-pearl. A compact case, a tortoise-shell comb and brush. And folded neatly and separated by tissue paper, layer after layer of dresses. Out of the trunk, one by one, Prof lifted a lime-green dinner dress, a short scarlet dress and a matching pair of open-toed high heels, and a black funeral dress and black veil. Finally, under one last layer of tissue paper, at the bottom of the trunk, a small hand purse containing some faded notes on the Bank of Lower Canada, a few hairpins, and a snapshot of a pretty, dark-complected young woman, smiling at the camera with an expression that was both demure and bold.

Prof drew in his breath. He passed one hand in front of his eyes, stared at the smiling girl again, then, with his hand shaking slightly, put the snapshot in his shirt pocket.

Still on his knees beside the trunk, holding the black dress and cloak across his arms as if he were holding the lifeless body of the beautiful young dressmaker herself, Prof looked up at Jim.

Jim nodded and turned away. Prof returned the dresses, toilet articles, scrapbooks, baseballs, and purse to the trunk and closed the lid. He got to his feet and looked at his pupil. "Let's get the hell away from here," he said.

5

Rivals

"Baseball Pliny" they called me in those days, and I was as proud of that as I was of the letters after my name. Oh, the rivalries! We fought John Reb to the death at Shiloh and Gettysburg, but we never hated him the way we did our opponents from the Landing. You could rely upon a battle royal erupting every time we played them. Why, half of the men and boys from both towns were slugging it out all over the common, and a fair number of womenfolk joining the affray as well.

—PLINY'S *HISTORY*

It's still very early in the morning but Crazy Kinneson, Jim's cousin, is already practicing on the outdoor court at the Academy playground, as he does every morning, winter and summer, fall and spring. Today Crazy's working on his crossover move to the basket. He starts about twenty feet out from the hoop with a head-fake right, then two low, fast dribbles diagonally to his left. Switches the ball to his right hand inches above the feet of Straw Man One: a worn-out broom taped bristles-up to the back of a battered metal chair to resemble an opponent with one hand raised on defense.

Crazy dips his left shoulder and blows by Straw Man One with two dribbles toward the hoop. But watch out, kiddo! Straw Man Two's camped in the lane directly in front of the basket, waiting to jam that lopsided old Wilson right down your throat. Not to worry, though. Head up, head always up, seeing the whole court in front of him the way Old Lady Benson, the town busybody, sees the entire village green from the porch of her second-story apartment over the *Monitor*, Crazy's spotted Two.

He pulls up just inside the free-throw line and oh, my, he's airborne. Up and up and up, releasing the ball in that moment of hang time when the shooter and all the world around him seem frozen in time like the grainy, black-and-white photograph of Crazy shooting his jumper in Jim's yearbook dedicated to his cousin: "To Philmore Kinneson. October 8, 1937–December 12, 1953. Our Hardwood Hero."

The villagers of Kingdom Common and Kingdom Landing had despised each other since time out of mind. As is often the case in these situations, the origin of the trouble was unclear. Of course, there were all kinds of explanations. All of these tales were lurid, and many were absurd. But no one, even Jim Kinneson's grandfather, knew for certain how the feud had started. Perhaps it dated all the way back to Gramp's father, Charles Kinneson II, rerouting the outlet of Lake Kingdom to flow north toward the Common.

In the summertime the Landing had something of the character of a resort community. Wealthy families from Boston and New York had vacationed at the Lake Kingdom House, a slightly down-at-the-heels summer hotel, for generations. Kingdom Common, for its part, was home to the American Furniture factory, and more of a mill town. Academy kids regarded their peers from the Landing as stuck-up. Landingites dismissed their enemies from the Academy as hicks.

It will come as no surprise to anyone who has ever lived in a small town to learn that the feud between the villages reached its peak each year during basketball season. The Academy gymnasium, especially, lent itself well to the rivalry. A cracker-box affair located in the basement of the school's south wing, it was less than half the size of a regulation basketball court. There was no out-of-bounds space around the perimeter. Players in-bounded the ball by placing a sneaker on the walls, which were flush with the sidelines. Sprained and even broken ankles were far from unheard of. Moreover, it was rumored that the north basket of the Academy gymnasium was only nine feet, ten inches high. The south basket was said to be ten feet, two inches. If so, the Academy players had no trouble making the adjustment. Not so their opponents, whose shots routinely bounced away long off the back of the north basket and fell short off the front of the south rim.

As for the fans, they crowded into a wraparound balcony overlooking the court below. Academy supporters usually sat in the east, north, and south bleachers. Away fans jammed themselves into the west balcony. Substitute players and coaches from both teams stood on the narrow flight of metal stairs leading down to the court from the south balcony. Commoners referred to the Academy gym as the fishbowl. Opponents called it the snake pit. Jim Kinneson, who covered the Common's home basketball games for the *Monitor*, sometimes referred to the gym in his articles as the "Coliseum."

For home games, Prof allowed the kids at the Academy to carry the pole from which the skeleton of Pliny Templeton was suspended from the science room down to the gym and stand it beside the scorer's table in the east balcony. Opposing players found the bones disconcerting. In this respect the former headmaster's yellowing old skeleton gave the Academy team one additional edge. Prof himself had once told the students during a pep rally that all was fair in love, war, and cross-county basketball rivalries.

"Dunk, dunk, dunk!" one hundred Academy kids yelled in unison.

It was the opening game of the season, with the Common hosting the Landing. The gym was already packed to overflowing as Jim's cousin Philmore "Crazy" Kinneson led his team onto the court. Jim, now a junior at the Academy, sat next to the scorer's table in the east balcony. He knew that Crazy wouldn't dunk the ball. Not just for show in the pregame warm-ups, anyway. Whatever else Crazy might be, he was no show-off.

Crazy's parents had died when he was a small boy, and he lived with his uncle, Punk Kinneson, the local dumpkeeper. About him at all times hung the acrid whiff of the dump fires that burned day and night year-round. Some of his classmates called him Smoky. At away games, fans taunted him with the name Goldilocks because of his bright yellow hair, which he wore long and tied back in a ponytail during the games. Most Commoners called him Crazy.

Not unusually skillful at other sports, with a basketball in his hands Jim's cousin was a magician. At five eleven he was rarely the tallest player on the court, but he had the build of a lumberjack and could leap like a catamount. Though his hands were as large and callused as a farmer's, Crazy had the softest shooting touch Jim had ever seen. His gently spinning jump shot fell through the net like a bird in flight settling into its nest.

On the court Crazy seemed to have a sixth sense. When an errant shot went up, he instantly divined the precise angle of the rebound. On defense his powers of anticipation were unequaled. You'd swear he knew where opponents intended to pass before they did. He'd spring out of nowhere to intercept the ball, then it was off to the races as he led the Academy's fast break down the floor, his golden ponytail flying.

A year ago the Harlem Globetrotters had come to Kingdom Common on their barnstorming tour. The Globetrotters had played an exhibition game against the local men's town team and the townies had recruited Crazy to play for them. Early on in the game Crazy'd begun to mimic the moves of the Trotters' star, Goose Tatum. If Goose bounced in a shot off the floor from fifteen feet away from the basket, so did Crazy. Goose shot free throws blindfolded and over his shoulder, passed the ball behind his back to himself off the clanging tin backboards. Crazy followed suit. Jim had gotten his best newspaper story to date out of the evening.

At the same time, some Commoners were a little afraid of Jim's cousin. He liked to walk through the village cemetery late at night; no one knew why. He referred to himself in the third person and was something of a gadfly. "Crazy wonders when you're going to start writing *real* stories, Jim," he said when Jim's Globetrotter piece appeared in the paper. He braced adults, as well. After Jim's father wrote an editorial excoriating both the Common and the Landing for voting down the bond issue for a much-needed new central school, Crazy buttonholed the editor on the sidewalk outside the *Monitor*. "Ah, Cousin Charles, my good man," he said. "Ever a prophet in your own country."

Jim liked Crazy and wasn't at all afraid of him. But he understood that, as his father periodically reminded him, his cousin bore watching. Not because he grew his hair long and smelled like burning tires. No. Crazy Kinneson bore watching because for all of his athletic renown, he was widely believed to be a fire starter. A pyromaniac, who could never be trusted with a pack of matches or a cigarette lighter.

Just in the last few weeks, several local sheds and abandoned barns had gone up in flames. Crazy'd been spotted at two of these fires. He'd even helped extinguish a small blaze at the disused Water of Life whiskey distillery on the edge of town before it could get out of hand. Jim was ashamed of himself for harboring suspicions about his eccentric cousin. Yet he couldn't help wondering. In 1882, the entire nearby border village of New Canaan, founded by Pliny Templeton and

Jim's great-grandfather Charles Kinneson II as a refuge for fugitive slaves, had been destroyed by a fire thought to have been deliberately set. Arson was no laughing matter in the Kingdom of Jim's youth, or in any other era.

"Take no prisoners, boys! Show no mercy!" roared Jim's older brother, Charlie, the Academy's varsity basketball coach, as the starting players lined up at center court for the opening jump ball. Though the Landing center was a good five inches taller, Crazy easily controlled the tap, batting it to his teammate Bobby LaBounty. Crazy cut hard for his basket, Bobby lobbed a perfect alley-oop pass back to him over two defenders, and Crazy laid the ball up and in uncontested. With Jim's cousin at center, the play was a reliably successful strategy for getting out to a quick lead. Charlie referred to it as the doldrums because it took the wind out of an opponent's sails.

Immediately the Common applied their seven-man press— the two extra defenders being the narrow side walls of the snake pit. Crazy picked off the Landing's inbound pass and drove hard toward his basket. Common, 4; Landing, 0.

From there the score seesawed as it usually did when the rivals played each other. Neither team was able to gain more than a five-point advantage. The much-taller Landing defense deviled Crazy fiercely, at times triple-teaming him.

"They're all over him, ref!" Coach Charlie hollered from his perch on the staircase. "Blow your Christly whistle."

Jim's father, Editor Kinneson, who was officiating the game with Prof Chadburn, blew his whistle. "Technical

foul," he said, pointing at Jim's brother and making the T
sign. In the west balcony the Landing fans roared with delight.

The first half ended with the Landing ahead by two. Despite the pressure defense, Crazy already had twenty of the
Common's twenty-five points. "Carrying his team on his
back," Jim scribbled in his reporter's notebook. Then he
crossed out the word "team" and wrote "town."

The school lobby was packed during halftime. The Academy seniors had set up two tables and were selling candy, popcorn and peanuts, and cold bottled drinks to raise funds for
their class trip. A temporary truce seemed to be in effect between the rival fans, though Jim noticed several glares and
overheard a few muttered remarks.

Next to the trophy case and directly across the lobby from
the front entrance of the Academy hung a life-size portrait of
the Reverend Dr. Pliny Templeton. In the painting the headmaster was standing at the top of the granite steps leading up
to the entrance, looking youthful and confident. He was wearing his academic robes, a tall man, well set up, with dark features and dark eyes full of intelligence and, Jim thought, humor
and kindness as well. The portrait had been painted in oils by
Gramp's long-deceased older sister, Mary Queen of Scots
Kinneson, a somewhat shadowy figure in the family tree.

It had been Jim's mother, Ruth Kinneson, who herself had
come to God's Kingdom from away, who had pointed out to
him the sorrowfulness behind the kindness and intelligence in
the eyes of Pliny's portrait. "I think he was always sad, Jimmy,"
Mom had said. "He was sad because he never did find his
wife. To him, she remained his beloved young bride sold off

down the river. He stayed in love with her all his life. The sorrow in his eyes, if I'm not just imagining it, is a measure of that love. Your great-aunt Mary captured it perfectly. Just the way you will someday when you write Pliny's life story."

Mom never doubted that Jim would go on to write the stories of God's Kingdom. In that regard Mom had explained something important to Jim about himself. With the increased self-awareness of adolescence, he had sometimes worried that he was too much of a daydreaming introvert—maybe partly in reaction to Charlie's flamboyance—to establish his own identity. True, he was captain of the Academy baseball team. He enjoyed the company of his classmates, even dated three or four of the girls from the Common. Yet his closest friend was his grown brother, and he gravitated toward Charlie's buds on the White Knights, and toward adults in general, often preferring the company of Gramp, Dad, and Mom to that of his contemporaries. Charlie said Jim had been born old, like their straitlaced Scottish ancestors. Recently, Jim had asked Mom if she thought he was too much of a loner. He confided to her that sometimes he thought he understood other people, family members and Commoners and even characters in the novels he devoured, better than he understood himself. Mom had put her hands on his shoulders and sat him down in a kitchen chair and looked him in the eye and said, "What you are, Jim, is a writer. You spend every waking moment writing. Even when you're reading a book or daydreaming, you're writing. *That's* your identity, sweetie."

"What's up, Kinneson? Dad K send his wet-behind-the-ears cub reporter out to cover the basketball game, did he?"

Mr. Gil Gilbert, the Academy shop teacher, had come up behind Jim while he was studying Pliny's portrait. Mr. Gilbert made a point of addressing male students by their last names. He referred to Jim, sneeringly, as a wet-behind-the-ears cub reporter or, more sneeringly still, as "Hemingway." Jim was quite certain that Mr. Gil Gilbert had never in his life read a book by Hemingway. He would not have been surprised to learn that Mr. Gilbert had not read any book at all in the last ten years.

"No," Jim said. "I'm writing a story about a teacher."

"Yeah? Who? That old colored boy in the painting?"

"The 'old colored boy' was very popular with his students," Jim said. "This guy I'm writing about, nobody can stand him."

"Go to hell, Hemingway. You're no more a writer than I'm the man in the moon."

"May I quote you on that?"

Mr. Gil Gilbert took a step forward. He had the red face of a heavy drinker, though so far as Jim knew he never touched a drop. "I bet you'd like to take a swing at me, wouldn't you, Hemingway? Be my guest. Give it your best shot."

Mr. Gil Gilbert was forever inviting his shop students to take a swing at him and give it their best shot. He disliked Jim in particular because some years ago, when Charlie was a student at the Academy, Mr. Gilbert had urged Jim's brother to take a swing at him and Charlie had promptly obliged him, breaking his jaw. At the moment, Jim would very much have liked to take Mr. Gil Gilbert up on his kind offer, but the shop teacher had spotted Frenchy Lamott across the lobby, wearing his cap inside the Academy, and was already stomping off to confiscate it.

The brush with Mr. Gilbert made Jim wonder. Why were so many teachers either beloved, like Prof Chadburn and Athena Allen, or detested, like Mr. Gil Gilbert and Miss Hark Kinneson? One thing was for sure. The Reverend Dr. Pliny Templeton had been beloved. You could see that in his portrait, too. Jim wished he knew more about him. In his great local history, Pliny had written very little about himself.

Feeling closed in, Jim jostled his way outside, onto the steps of the school. The Landing team bus was parked across the green under a streetlight, where it was less apt to be vandalized. The driver and a local deputy sheriff stood vigil beside it, stamping their feet in the frosty night. High above the village the December moon looked small and drained of color.

Jim glanced at the playground beside the Academy, dimly illuminated in the moonlight. He thought of Crazy, practicing day in and day out on the bent and netless playground hoop, even on the coldest winter mornings when the temperature in God's Kingdom fell to forty-five and sometimes fifty degrees below zero.

"Hey, Jimmy," someone yelled from the doorway behind him. "Second half's starting."

Partway through the third quarter, the Landing began to figure out the Academy's defense. On three consecutive possessions, they turned the Common's full-court press into their own fast break, scoring easy baskets each time. Charlie called time and took off the press.

The editor and Prof officiated tightly to keep the game from getting away from them. At the same time, they let the kids play hard. "Come on, call it!" Charlie continued to bellow each time the Landing players collapsed on Crazy to deny him the ball or a lane to the basket.

Crazy didn't rattle. Playing always within himself, never overreaching, he found the open man under the basket, whipped the ball back outside to an unguarded teammate, sprinted outside himself and launched his long, deadly jumpers over a screen.

With the Landing up by two and just seconds remaining in the fourth quarter, Bobby LaBounty made a thread-the-needle bounce pass into Crazy at low post. Instantly the big center and two forwards from the Landing swarmed him. There was no place for Jim's cousin to go. But with his back to the basket, Crazy leaped high above the three defenders, spun around in midair, and executed the first two-handed slam dunk ever seen in the Kingdom.

As the buzzer ending the game sounded, the editor cupped one hand upside down and dipped it sharply to indicate that Crazy'd gotten his shot off in time. The basket counted. The fourth quarter had ended with the score tied and the game was going into overtime.

Or was it? Prof and the editor were conferring at midcourt. Prof looked up at the scorer's table and lifted his index finger. "Plus one," he shouted out over the terrific din in the gymnasium. "He was fouled in the act of shooting." Crazy had a final free throw coming. With it he could win the game.

From the Landing fans in the west balcony came an anguished howl rising to a crescendo of pure outrage. The Commoners responded with thunderous applause. Crazy stepped up to the foul line, bounced the ball once, and lifted it to his one-handed shooting position. He seemed oblivious to the furor in the balconies. Crazy shot one hundred free throws a day on the playground hoop. In his entire varsity career he hadn't missed half a dozen foul shots.

Just as Crazy bent his knees to shoot, someone in the Landing balcony flung a handful of Good & Plenties onto the court. Some of the hard little pink and white candies struck Crazy. Others bounced off the floor and skittered across it to the opposite wall. Crazy glanced up at the shrieking fans.

"Pyro!" a voice screamed out. "Crazy pyro bastard."

Suddenly the air was full of missiles. Green, red, and yellow Dots. Canada mints. Black Crows, candy corn, more Good & Plenties, flying from balcony to balcony. Some seemed aimed at Crazy himself. A three-ring binder struck his leg. A lunch box narrowly missed his head.

The editor and Prof ran to Crazy's side, held up their hands, and shouted at the mob to stop throwing things. Crazy continued to stand at the foul line, knees slightly bent, the ball cradled in his big hands just above his head. Then he lowered the ball and set it down on the line.

In a blizzard of popcorn, hard and soft candies, peanuts and peanut shells, with his hands held up to his eyes like horse blinders, Crazy turned and walked across the gym floor toward the stairs at the far end of the court. Shielding his eyes, he glanced back over his shoulder once, as if checking to be sure that the ball was still where he left it.

As Crazy continued toward the stairs, an empty pop bottle, bright and flashing, caught him flush on the left temple. All Jim could be sure of was that the flying glass bottle had come from somewhere behind him in the home balcony. Crazy sank to his knees as if to pray. Then he crumpled sideways onto the court.

The gym fell deathly quiet.

Whoever threw the pop bottle that killed Jim's cousin was never charged. Maybe the bottle was meant for the Landing-ites and slipped out of the thrower's hand. No one ever came forward to testify, much less accept responsibility for the boy's death. In an editorial in *the Monitor* entitled "The Stoning of Philmore Kinneson," Jim's father wrote that it was the feud itself that had killed Crazy, and the two towns should be prosecuted for murder.

The entire Common seemed to turn out for Crazy Kinneson's funeral. Donors came together to commission a granite tombstone in his memory, with a regulation-size, carved granite basketball on top. But Crazy's story didn't end there. One snowy evening several weeks after his death the defunct distillery caught fire again. This time it burned to the ground. That same night the Lake Kingdom House in the Landing, closed for the winter, went up in flames.

"At least they can't lay these latest fires to Crazy's door," Jim told his father the next morning.

"Don't be too sure about that, James," the editor said, and as usual, he was right. At first each village blamed its most recent fire on its rival. But the blackened ruins of the distillery and the old resort hotel were still smoking when a new rumor began to fly through the towns. Crazy's ghost had returned to God's Kingdom and set the fires.

Jim's father summed it up in a second editorial. "We needed a hero and a scapegoat," he wrote. "Philmore Kinneson was unfortunate enough to be both, in life and in death."

6

Only in the Kingdom

With the help of a red ox named Samson, Charles II and I built the Academy from pink, or "Scotch," granite blocks quarried on Canada Mountain by stonecutters from New Canaan. Except for Samson, whose task it was to turn a bull wheel atop a platform reached by a series of inclined ramps, and thereby raise the one-ton granite blocks, we had very little assistance, but dozens and even scores of superintendents, and you may be sure that not one thing Charles or Samson or I did was right. At last the walls were erected. But imagine our astonishment, and the gleeful delight of the superintendents, when Samson refused to descend the ramps to terra firma. Sadly, we were constrained to butcher the poor beast on high, whereupon we held a great, free ox roast on the Common at which about half of our self-anointed superintendents declared that we had burned the beef, the other half that the meat was so bloody underdone they could not lay a lip over it.

—PLINY'S *HISTORY*

Mike the Moose appeared on the village green in the bottom of the ninth inning of the opening game of the Northern Vermont Town Team League between Kingdom Common and Kingdom Landing. There were two outs and the Common was behind by a run, with Jim Kinneson on first base and his cousin Job "Moose" Kinneson, the team's cleanup hitter, at bat. Everyone's attention was riveted on the game so nobody saw exactly where Mike had come from. There he was, moseying in past the hometown bleachers along the first-base line as though he'd just fallen out of the sky.

The Landing's closer, a raw-boned logger with a frighteningly errant fastball, had just brushed Moose back from the plate with a head-high pitch six inches inside. Moose was a good-natured giant, but as Jim's older brother, Charlie, had told him, beware the wrath of a patient man. He pointed the business end of his forty-inch Louisville Slugger at the pitcher. "Don't do that again, old son," he said.

The pitcher went into his stretch. He checked Jim, who had a shorter lead than usual, and no intention of taking the bat out of the hands of his team's best hitter by getting picked off. That's when Jim's dad, Editor Kinneson, umping behind the plate, spotted Mike.

"Time, gentlemen!" The editor threw up his hands and stepped out from behind the catcher. He pointed at the three-quarters-grown bull moose, now standing near the Outlaws' on-deck circle as if waiting for his turn to bat.

"Why, looky there," Moose said. "It's a moose."

From the bleachers, laughter. Charlie liked to refer to Job Kinneson as the master of the obvious. At six-six and two hundred and forty pounds, Moose was the best long-ball hitter in the league. He owned a small dairy farm on the county road, just outside the village. Weekends he filled in as an auxiliary deputy sheriff at local events requiring the presence of a police officer. The master of the obvious could take the air out of a dance-hall slugfest just by walking through the door.

Moose had a tiny, loud wife from Maine, known in the Common as Mrs. Moose, and five large, loud daughters, ranging in age from six to twelve, whom he referred to as "the gals." Mrs. Moose and the gals never missed one of Moose's home games. When Mike showed up on the green, they were perched in the bucket loader on the front of Moose's green John Deere farm tractor next to the first-base bleachers, rooting for their father to bust one into the street in front of the brick shopping block and win the game.

"You gals stay put," Moose called over to them. To the moose he said, "Keep off the playing field, young fella. We've got a ball game to finish here."

As Moose liked to put it, he had a way with critters. When someone in the Kingdom found an orphaned beaver kit or an injured fawn, they'd bring it to him to raise. He knew how to heal hawks with broken wings. Once he adopted a motherless bear cub. When it nipped off his left index finger at the middle knuckle during a play fight, he gave it to the Quebec provincial zoo across the border.

Moose pointed at Mike with his abbreviated forefinger. "Stay," he said.

Mike, for his part, knelt down on his front legs, as moose will sometimes do in a hay field, and began to crop the short grass near the first-base coaching box.

"Good moose," Moose said. Then he stepped back into

the batter's box and poled the next pitch over the bandstand in deep center field for a game-winning home run.

No gloater, Moose ducked his head and started around the bases with his eyes on the ground. As he jogged toward first, the gals swarmed him. They clung to his legs and scrambled onto his shoulders, shrieking joyously. Just behind them came Mike, ambling along and from time to time giving Moose an encouraging reef with its modest set of antlers. Jim crossed home plate, where the team had gathered to greet him and Moose, then ran for his reporter's camera in the dugout. His shot of Moose rounding third base with the gals hanging off him like young possums in pinafores and Mike tagging along behind made the front page of that week's *Monitor*. A second photo of Moose driving his John Deere past the courthouse with Mrs. Moose in the seat beside him, the gals riding in the bucket, and Mike bringing up the rear appeared on the sports page with Jim's account of the game.

"Uh-oh, boys," Cousin Stub Kinneson, the team's second baseman, said as Moose's outfit, now including Mike, proceeded up the street. "Here comes trouble in a big hat."

Warden R. W. Kinneson came striding along the sidewalk from the courthouse. He cut off Moose's entourage at the northeast corner of the Common. "Just where do you think you're taking that animal?" Cousin R. W. said.

"The gals here have named him Mike," Moose said to the warden. "Mike the Moose. I'm not taking him anywhere. He seems to have muckled onto me. I believe he thinks I'm his mother."

The warden jutted his hat up at Moose. Jim snapped a picture. A crowd was beginning to gather.

"See here, cousin," R. W. said. "That beast never would have ventured into town if it didn't have brain-worm disease. I'm going to have to destroy it."

Instantly all five of the large little gals burst into tears.

"Hear them, won't you," Moose said.

R. W. took a step toward Mike and unbuckled his holster strap. Moose got down off the John Deere and stood between Mike and the warden.

"Job Kinneson, I'm warning you. You're preventing an officer of the law from carrying out his sworn duty."

"Mike's a good moose," Moose said. "He's taken a shine to us, is all. You gals quieten down now. Nobody's going to shoot anybody."

"You haven't heard the last of this," the warden said.

Moose climbed back up on the John Deere and headed home with Mike trailing along behind.

"*State of Vermont vs. Job Kinneson*," the county prosecutor, Zack Barrows, announced the following Wednesday at the weekly arraignments at the courthouse.

Warden R. W. Kinneson stood beside Zack at the prosecutor's table. Moose Kinneson and his attorney, Jim's brother, Charlie, stood at the defense table across the aisle.

Jim sat in the third row of benches behind the defense table, pencil and notebook at the ready. This was his first court

assignment for the *Monitor*. Feeling proud but nervous, he jot-
ted down some details to add atmosphere to his story. The
light globes hanging on metal rods from the stamped-tin
ceiling. The four tall windows in the west wall, overlooking
the village common. The worn hardwood floor and benches.

Most interesting of all to Jim was the mural covering the
entire front wall of the courtroom. It was called *The Seven
Wonders of God's Kingdom*, and had been painted by Gramp's
older sister, Mary Queen of Scots Kinneson, at about the
same time that she painted the life-size portrait of Pliny Templeton that hung in the foyer of the Academy. In the most vi-
vacious colors, and with astonishing verisimilitude, Mary had
depicted, from left to right across the wall, the High Falls behind the Common Hotel, Pliny's great granite Academy, the
Île d'Illusion in Lake Memphremagog, the baseball diamond
on the village green, Pliny's *History of Kingdom County* open
to the narrative of Lake Runaway running away down the
Lower Kingdom Valley, Jay Peak at the height of the fall foli-
age season, and the second-longest covered bridge in the world,
at the southern gateway to the Kingdom, where Abolition Jim
and his fellow secessionists had been wiped out by federal
troops.

Soon after completing the mural, Mary Kinneson, not yet
seventeen, had dropped out of the Academy and run off to live
with the descendants of the fugitive slaves who had founded
New Canaan, on the Canadian side of the Upper Kingdom
River. Gramp had scarcely known her. Mary had died when
he was five, in the Great Forest Fire of 1882 that had killed
nearly a hundred residents of New Canaan.

As usual, Judge Forrest Allen, Athena Allen's father, was presiding. Judge Allen conducted his courtroom in an avuncular manner but didn't suffer fools or brook impertinence. Recently, he'd been in the hospital with heart problems. This morning he looked tired.

"Judge Allen," Zack said, "the state is charging Mr. Job Kinneson with interfering with an officer acting in the line of duty. Also with illegally taking a protected wild animal. The animal in question is a young moose. Warden Kinneson has reason to believe that the moose has brain-worm disease. Brain-worm is highly contagious. If it's transferred to deer, it's invariably fatal. The State needs to confiscate this animal and put it down so it can be tested in accordance with the law of the land."

"Your honor," Charlie said, "my client, Mr. Job Kinneson, is an auxiliary deputy sheriff and well acquainted with the law of the land. He didn't 'take' the moose in question anywhere. It followed him home. Moose put it into his lower pasture with his young stock because it isn't quite ready to fend for itself. There's nothing at all wrong with it other than it misses its mother. Mike, that's the moose's name, seems to have adopted Moose as his surrogate mother. It's very touching, actually."

Judge Forrest Allen did not appear to be touched. He gave Charlie a weary look. "From where?" he said.

"I'm sorry, your honor? From where?"

"You said the moose followed Job home. From where did it follow him home?"

"It appeared on the village green during our baseball game

with the Landing. Moose had just walloped a walk-off home run over the bandstand and—"

"Excuse me, Charlie. Let me understand this. The moose in question hit a home run? Surely you don't expect me to believe that, even in the Kingdom, moose play town-team baseball?"

Jim was writing fast.

"No, your honor, of course not. Moose Kinneson hit the home run. Mike the Moose just ran the bases with him. Mike was on first at the time and when Moose rounded the bag, Mike followed him."

"Mike was playing first base?"

"No, your honor. He was eating the grass near the coaching box."

"Charlie, I have warned you often before. The Eighth District Court of Vermont is not an Abbott and Costello production. Appearances to the contrary notwithstanding, this is an arraignment in a court of law. You do understand that, don't you?"

"Yes, your honor. That's why I'm requesting a summary ruling from the bench to dismiss these frivolous charges. This is a tempest in a teapot. I'm prepared to prove it. Defense requests permission to call one special witness."

"This isn't a trial, Charlie. Witnesses don't usually testify at arraignments."

"It won't take two minutes."

The judge passed his hand over his robe in the region of his heart. "I'll give you exactly sixty seconds. And Charlie? Don't push your luck. I have had just about a sufficiency, this morning, of moose and of Kinnesons."

The judge looked at his watch. "Fifty-five seconds."

"Thank you, your honor. I'll be right back." Charlie walked quickly to the rear of the courtroom and out the door. A moment later he returned with Mrs. Moose, leading Mike by a halter. "Go ahead, Moose," Charlie called down to Job Kinneson at the defense table.

Moose whistled. "Here, Mike."

Mike trotted down the center aisle. As he neared the front of the courtroom, he noisily deposited a heap of moose pellets beside the prosecutor's table.

"Moose, would you kindly walk to the back of the courtroom?" Charlie said.

Moose started back down the aisle. Mike came along behind him like a bird dog at heel. When they reached the door, Mrs. Moose led Mike back out into the hall.

Charlie said, "I submit, your honor, that this moose is perfectly healthy. It most certainly doesn't have brain-worm disease."

"Warden Kinneson," the judge said. "Can't you just take that animal out in the woods and let it go? It looks plenty big enough to care for itself to me."

"I expect it would only come back, your honor. Besides which, if it transfers brain-worm to so much as one wild deer, there goes Vermont's whitetail population, down the drain. And a big chunk of Vermont's economy right along with it."

"Well, R.W., you may be surprised to learn that I am more concerned with the laws of the state of Vermont than with its economy. So I am going to take all of this information under advisement. I will have a ruling within a week. In the meantime,

I am remanding young Mike back to Job Kinneson's farm.
In his capacity as auxiliary deputy sheriff, Job will keep Mike
under house arrest, with no contact with Vermont's precious
deer herd."

"Thank you, your honor," Charlie said.

"Next case," Judge Allen said.

Editor Kinneson blue-penciled the atmospheric descrip-
tions out of Jim's article on Moose's arraignment. "Save that
for your storywriting, James," he said. "This is the weekly
court news, not *War and Peace*."

Charlie told Jim he was confident that Judge A would hand
down a ruling favorable to Moose and Mike. Even if the judge
refused Charlie's request for a summary dismissal and allowed the case to go to trial, no Kingdom jury would ever vote
to destroy Mike.

But on the day after the arraignment, Judge Allen experi-
enced more chest pain and was taken to the hospital in Memphremagog. The judge's caseload was transferred to a
middle-aged magistrate from Burlington, a former U.S. Marine major, who promptly threw out the charges that Moose
had interfered with the warden. In the same ruling, the ex-
leatherneck decreed that, in the interest of protecting the deer
herd, Warden R. W. Kinneson and the Vermont Fish and
Wildlife Department had the right to put Mike down and run
their tests.

Warden Kinneson bided his time. He waited until Moose
was away with his John Deere, mowing a sick neighbor's hay-

field. Then the warden descended on Moose's place with two state troopers and a sheriff's deputy. It was publication day at the *Monitor,* and Jim was folding papers as they came off the press when he happened to look out the large front window with the words *Kingdom County Monitor* written backwards on the inside of the glass and see the cavalcade leaving the village: R. W. in his forest-green warden's truck, the troopers in marked cruisers, the deputy in a sheriff department's van ordinarily used to transport prisoners. The editor, at his desk near the window, saw them, too. He tossed Jim the keys to his DeSoto. "Go," he said.

Jim arrived just as the deputy and one of the troopers were fastening a rope with a loop in the middle around Mike's neck. Each of the two officers held one end of the rope to prevent Mike from bolting. The other trooper held Mrs. Moose. The large little gals shrieked. Warden R. W. Kinneson got his .30-30 and a chain saw from his truck. He set down the saw, took aim with the rifle, and shot Mike squarely between the eyes at point-blank range. Then he started his chain saw, drowning out the screams of Mrs. Moose and the gals, severed Mike's head, and drove off with it in the bed of his pickup.

Moose, who'd heard the rifle shot from half a mile away, arrived home on the John Deere a few minutes later to discover the gals wailing beside Mike's headless carcass. Mrs. Moose had told them that Mike was in moose heaven, but they were having none of it. "He is not in heaven," the eldest child shouted. "He's laying in the barnyard dead as a doornail. Now Papa's going to shoot the warden and go to the electric chair."

"No one's going to the electric chair," Moose said. "Let's give Mikey a decent burial out back of the barn. You gals can dress up in your Sunday school clothes."

While Mrs. Moose took the girls into the house to dress for the funeral, Jim got a photograph of Moose scooping Mike into the John Deere's bucket. "Do you have anything to say, Moose?" Jim asked.

"To say?" Moose said. "No, Jimmy. The gals can say something at the graveside service if they want to. Then the time for saying things will be over."

The editor declined to run Jim's shot of the headless moose in the tractor bucket. He said that the photograph of the warden drawing a bead on Mike with his rifle from two feet away, while the police restrained Mike with a rope around his neck, told the entire story. The editor let Jim's caption stand. "The Execution of Mike the Moose."

Jim wanted to headline his accompanying story "Only in the Kingdom." His father said no. He told Jim that this kind of overreaching on the part of the state happened everywhere. "It doesn't matter where you live, Jim. Vermont. Idaho. It's pretty much the same everywhere. You can't beat city hall."

"You've spent your whole career fighting city hall, Dad."

"I have," the editor said. "And very rarely beaten them."

Moose dropped off the baseball team. He quit coming to practice and didn't show up at games. On a couple of occasions Jim pestered him into hitting him a few grounders on the green, but he could tell that Moose's heart wasn't in it. The sheriff's department no longer called him to cover barn dances and fairs. When Ben Currier brought Moose an abandoned fawn still in its spots, Moose told him to take it to the vet in Memphremagog.

Moose still drove his John Deere into town but he didn't sign up for the tractor pull at the Kingdom Fair. Sometimes, after running his errands at the feed store and hardware, he'd back up to the east side of the green across the street from the courthouse and watch the people going in and out of the sheriff's office. One morning Jim asked him what he was doing there. "Waiting," Moose said.

At the time, Jim was on his way to take a picture for that week's *Monitor* of a local law-enforcement personnel meeting. The officers were getting together at the sheriff's headquarters for a training session on community-police relations. As Jim and Moose watched from across the street, two state police cruisers pulled into the courthouse parking lot beside three sheriff's department vehicles, a border-patrol car, and Warden Kinneson's green pickup.

"You know what those rigs over there put me in mind of, Jimmy?" Moose said. "The little tin ducks that go floating by in the shooting gallery at the fair." Moose started the John Deere. He looked both ways, then drove it across the street at what Jim would later describe in the *Monitor* as "an unhurried rate of speed." Jim's article went on to describe how Moose, at the helm of the tractor, drove down the row of parked law-enforcement vehicles, smashing in the hood and roof of each one with the front-end bucket, then methodically backed the John Deere up and over the patrol cars and the warden's truck, reducing Kingdom County's entire fleet of police vehicles to a heap of crushed scrap metal.

This time Jim's father let him headline his story "Only in the Kingdom." Where else would an aggrieved farmer and former auxiliary deputy sheriff use a tractor with a front-end bucket loader as his weapon of choice to avenge the wrongful death of an overgrown cousin of a deer? Jim captioned the two photos that ran on the front page with his article "Sitting Ducks Before" and "Sitting Ducks After."

The new judge remanded Job Kinneson to the state hospital in Waterbury for evaluation to determine whether he was mentally fit to stand trial. The AP wire service picked up Jim's "Only in the Kingdom" story, giving the young reporter his first national byline. Letters to the editor in the *Monitor* ran nine out of ten in support of Moose, though a few local boosters complained that Jim's article had given the Kingdom a bad name. "Welcome to the newspaper business, son," the editor said.

One day the following week Charlie received a telephone call from the state hospital. The official who called was not very forthcoming, but Charlie gathered that Moose had come across several attendants subduing an unruly inmate and had "gone off." Moose was tranquilized, then referred for electric shock treatment. The next day he'd escaped the hospital grounds.

Charlie alerted Mrs. Moose, who said that no doubt Moose would show up at home in a day or two. He didn't, though. He didn't show up anywhere. Job Kinneson vanished as if he'd fallen off the edge of the earth.

Cruelest of all were the false sightings. Someone would be certain he'd spotted Moose ice fishing on Pond in the Sky. Or boxing on the county fair circuit in New Hampshire. Somebody else heard he was playing semipro baseball on Cape Cod. Charlie checked out each report. Nothing.

Eventually, Mrs. Moose sold the farm, herd, and machinery, including the John Deere, to Ben Currier, and returned to Maine with the gals to live with her parents. Years passed. Then, in one of those entirely unpredictable yet, in retrospect, inevitable-seeming turns of events, the mystery of Moose Kinneson's disappearance solved itself. As part of the nationwide deinstitutionalization movement, the Vermont State Hospital began shutting down its wards and reassigning patients to group homes and foster families in their own communities. Finally, the hospital closed altogether.

As the brushy back fields of the property where the inmates had once cultivated a small farm were being cleared and leveled for an apartment complex, workers discovered an unmarked graveyard. In it were the remains of several dozen people, including a number of newborn infants. Many of the bodies showed signs of traumatic injuries. The state forensics lab concluded that more than half of the graveyard's occupants had died violently, including the six foot six male of about thirty-five with a crushed skull and a partly missing left index finger.

Now Mrs. Moose and the grown gals seemed to have vanished. Her parents had died, she'd remarried and moved again, and Charlie and Jim were unable to trace her or the gals. The brothers claimed the long skeleton with the missing forefinger. One summer afternoon when the orange hawkweed and black-eyed Susans were in bloom, a day much like the day when Mike the Moose had appeared on the village green, Charlie and Jim attended Moose's interment in the village cemetery. Other than the backhoe operator who dug the grave, no one else was present to see the remains of the former longball hitter laid to rest.

"Should we say a word?" Charlie said after the backhoe had filled in Moose's grave and gone away.

Jim thought for a minute. Then he shook his head. "Only in the Kingdom," he said.

Charlie waited for his brother to continue, but Jim didn't. What else was there to say? Even Charlie couldn't think of another thing.

7

False Spring

In God's Kingdom, family and work are all-important. Every-thing else, even religion, falls into one or both of these two categories.

—PLINY'S *HISTORY*

I t was the late fall of Jim's junior year at the Academy, and for the first time in more than a century, false spring had come to God's Kingdom. Two months ago, the elm trees around the perimeter of the village common had turned yel-low, then dropped their leaves and gone dormant. Just yester-day Jim had noticed that the elms were putting out tiny golden leaves again. Last night he'd heard a flock of geese headed north, as if confused by the open cornfields and unseasonably warm weather. Yesterday was the fifth consecutive afternoon that the squat, old-fashioned Coca-Cola-bottle thermometer on the door of Quinn's drugstore had hit eighty degrees, with Thanksgiving now just a day away.

Driving up the one-lane track on Kingdom Mountain in

the dawn mist, Jim noticed other signs of false spring. The popple trees growing up in brushy fields of long-abandoned farmsteads were pale yellow with new catkins. An easy rain overnight had given the few remaining pastures the emerald sheen you will see in the spring in the countryside of Ireland and of Kingdom County and nowhere else. The roadside stream off the mountain was up and milky from the rain.

"It's shortened the winter by a week," Dad had said last night at supper. "False spring."

"Maybe so," Gramp said. "But we'll pay for it later on."

It was an unsettled season in an uneasy era in the Kingdom. Family farms were going under one after another. An early influenza epidemic was sweeping through the county. Most Commoners blamed the flu on the strange weather. Long-married couples were short with each other; schoolchildren were restless. What should they do? Get up a late-November game of flies and grounders on the village green? Deer hunters who came to the Kingdom from away each fall sat drinking coffee in the hotel dining room and grousing about the absence of tracking snow. Not, as Gramp said, that a single man jack of them could track a herd of wooly mammoths the width of the green in three feet of fresh snow.

This was an especially frustrating morning for Jim. Gramp and Dad and Charlie had gone off to deer camp without him for the first time since he'd begun going with them. Though Jim didn't hunt deer himself any longer, going to camp with the men in his family was his favorite annual activity. In the Kingdom, deer camp was more about family than hunting, but the day before, as the men were getting ready to head out, the letter had arrived from Miss Jane, summoning Jim to her farm on Kingdom Mountain:

> *Dear James,*
> *I will require your assistance tomorrow morning regarding a family matter. Kindly meet me at eight o'clock A.M. sharp, in my barnyard.*
>
> > *Your cousin,*
> > *Jane Kinneson*

Miss Jane Kinneson was Gramp's first cousin, and therefore Jim's cousin as well, though several times removed. For many decades she had operated a small farm on the mountain. She was also a well-known bird carver and wood sculptor. She had even sculpted life-size, wooden figures of her Kinneson ancestors, and arranged them throughout her farmhouse, to keep herself company. Miss Jane referred to the carved family members as her people. As a small boy, Jim had been somewhat afraid of them.

During haying season, and again at maple-sugaring time, Jim assisted Miss Jane on her farm on the mountain. He helped her get up her winter's wood, spade her garden plot, and bank her farmhouse with evergreen boughs for cold weather. Miss Jane had a sharp tongue, and was difficult to please. It was rumored that she had been disappointed in love. Some Commoners claimed that she had second sight and could predict the future.

Miss Jane relished the old ways and expressions of her ancestors. Like Gramp, she was a born storyteller. Though it often seemed to Jim that he could never do anything right in Jane's eyes, she had always encouraged him with his own story-writing. "If you're writing, you're a writer," she said. "If you aren't writing, you aren't a writer. You've been writing since you were five, James. That makes you a writer."

Miss Jane was a writer herself. For decades she had been rewriting the King James Bible. In Miss Jane's *Kingdom Mountain Bible,* God didn't turn Lot's wife into a pillar of salt to punish her for a moment's curiosity. He didn't flood out His own creation, or stand idly by while the Roman soldiers hammered His own begotten son up on a wooden cross. No-where in the New Testament of the *Kingdom Mountain Bible* did Jesus curse a fig tree, or any other living thing. Nor did He command His disciples to turn their backs on their parents and wives and children. To Jane Hubbell Kinneson of King-dom Mountain, family was everything.

Jane stood waiting in her barnyard beside Black Hawk, her elderly Morgan driving horse. She wore her red-and-black wool hunting jacket over a long black dress, and was toting her father's Civil War rifle. It occurred to Jim that the tableau of Jane with the rifle, standing near her horse, her weathered barn attached to her weathered house by a series of ramshackle weathered sheds in the background, could itself have been a daguerreotype from the Civil War era. Kingdom Moun-tain, looming in the background, might have been a peak in the Blue Ridge or Great Smokies, Jane the matriarch of an outlier family from some Kentucky hollow an unlucky stranger might wander into, never to be seen again.

This morning Black Hawk was hitched to Jane's high-sided hay wagon. Lashed upright with bailing twine to the open-slatted sides of the wagon were several of Miss Jane's carved wooden people, including Charles Kinneson I, in a painted-on buckskin jacket and leggings; James I, the secessionist, bearing the green Kingdom Republic flag, with a leaping brook trout embroidered on it; and Gramp's father, Charles "Mad Charlie" II. Beside Charles II was a carved black man wearing a dark suit and a clerical collar. The black man, of course, was Pliny Templeton. Jim also recognized, in the hay wagon, his Abenaki great-great-great-grandmother Molly Molasses, Charles I's wife; Jane's father, Supreme Court Justice Morgan Kinneson; and several other Kinneson forbears. Why they were tied in the wagon, and what Jane intended to do with them this morning, Jim had no idea. On the bed of the wagon were two shovels, a pickax, and a grave blanket woven from spruce and fir boughs. Cradled in the evergreen blanket was Jane's black lunch pail.

Jim nodded at the rifle. "Are you going to shoot a deer if we see one?"

"Hardly," Jane said.

She clicked to Black Hawk, who started up the lane behind the house and barn. The wagon bounced over the ruts as Black Hawk pulled it up the slope past blossoming dandelions and cowslips. The horse was gray around the muzzle. Once Jane had kept two stocky Canadian workhorses for plowing and haying, harvesting corn, and gathering maple sap. She'd milked a dozen Jerseys and raised chickens and hogs. Lately, as her dairy herd and other animals had died off, Jane had not replaced them. Except for a barn cat, Black Hawk was the last domestic animal on her farmstead. Jim thought that the Morgan was about twenty-five. He'd learned to ride on him.

A silvery rill, brimful from the rain the night before, poured off the slope beside the lane. Along the brook, fluorescent-green skunk's cabbages were poking up. Jim's English class had been reading *Macbeth*. He pointed at the skunk's cabbage. "The times are out of joint," he said.

"When haven't they been?" Miss Jane said. "Up here in God's Kingdom, when have the times not been out of joint?"

And, higher on the mountainside, "How are you getting on with your storywriting, James?"

Jim said he was just finishing a new story inspired by Pliny Templeton's account of Gramp's father, Charles II, rerouting the outlet of Lake Runaway and flooding out the Lower Kingdom Valley.

As they continued up the lane, Jane said, "You know, of course, that's how Charles II met his future wife, Eliza Kittredge. Without so much as a by-your-leave, Charles appropriated the Kittredges' plough horse to ride down the valley ahead of the cresting flood and warn the people in its path. When he returned the horse, she fell in love with him, though they didn't get married until some years later. First he ran away to the Mexican War to avoid being tarred and feathered, or worse, for the damage done by the flood. Shall we have a quick round of Connection, James?"

Connection was a game Miss Jane had invented for the purpose of teaching Jim local history. She'd name two seemingly unrelated events, often decades or even centuries apart. To win the game, Jim had to explain how the events were directly connected by an unbroken chain of cause and effect.

"What is the connection between my uncle Charlie's rerouting the outlet of Lake Runaway and your college education?"

"I guess I don't know," Jim said.

"Why, certainly you know. On his way back from Mexico, Charles met Pliny in New Orleans. He helped Pliny escape from slavery, and paid for his education at the state university. Years later, the university established the Templeton Scholarship, to be awarded annually to the top-ranking graduate of Pliny's Academy. In two years, that will be you."

Jim grinned. "How do you know? Second sight?"

"No one knows the future, me least of all," Jane said. "But I should be greatly disappointed in you, James, greatly disappointed indeed, if you do not win the Templeton Scholarship."

They continued up the lane together to the family cemetery where Jane's ancestors were buried. She unhooked Black Hawk from the traces and turned him loose to graze along the edge of the rill, where the grass was greening again in the false spring. She told Jim there was no need to hobble the horse. He was too old to stray very far.

Just outside the pointed iron fence stakes surrounding her ancestors' plots, Jane began digging in the thin mountain topsoil. Jim picked up the second shovel and joined her. It crossed his mind that she might intend to bury her wooden people, though why, he couldn't imagine. Here and there inside the fence, spring beauties were blossoming. For years, on May Day, Miss Jane had recruited Jim to help her pick spring beauties for the miniature sweetgrass flower baskets she left hanging on the front doorknobs of friends' houses in the Common. Miss Jane noticed the blooming flowers, too. She shook her head. Mayflowers in late November.

A couple of feet down, they hit blue clay. Miss Jane exchanged her shovel for the pickax, loosening the hardpan for Jim to spade out of the deepening trench. In places, they encountered pockets of shale and shards of slate.

By noon they had opened up a hole about eight feet long, four feet wide, and five or six feet deep. To Jim it looked large enough to accommodate Jane's people, if that was her plan.

Out of her black lunch pail Jane produced deviled-egg sandwiches on homemade salt-rising bread; a pound wedge of cheddar cheese, aged for five years in her root cellar; a paper sack of Vermont common crackers; two stone jars of sweet cider from the old-fashioned apple orchard beside her farmhouse; and her specialty, molasses cartwheel cookies. Jane gave Black Hawk a feedbag. After last night's rain there was plenty of drinking water for him in the nearby rivulet, which sounded like it did in April, a steady background murmuring that Jim heard without listening to it.

"You are, of course, wondering what Pliny, who grew up on a tobacco plantation in Kentucky, was doing in Louisiana," Jane said in the matter-of-fact tone in which she delivered her prescient observations. "So I'll give you a chance to redeem yourself. What is the connection between Pliny's loss of his hand in Kentucky and his appearance in Louisiana six months later?"

"I don't know how he got to New Orleans. Gramp told me Pliny never talked about his missing hand, or anything else from his life in slavery. Gramp said Pliny's master probably cut off his hand to punish him."

"Pliny's master did no such thing, James. What he did do, however, was worse yet. One evening Pliny returned from the fields to discover that his young wife had been sold down the river."

"My God!" Jim said.

Jane continued her story. "Pliny loved his wife more than life itself, James. To prevent him from running after her, his owner chained him by the wrist to the boiler of a wrecked steamboat that he used for an impromptu jail. That's when Pliny made his great covenant with God. He got down on his knees and closed his eyes and told God if He'd let him search for his wife—he didn't say *find* her, James; Pliny figured that was up to God, not him—if God would free Pliny from that boiler so he could search for her, Pliny would dedicate the rest of his life to preaching God's word and doing His works. When he opened his eyes, the first thing he spotted was an old ax with a broken-off helve."

"I don't understand," Jim said. "You said he was chained to the boiler. You can't cut through a chain with an ax."

"No," Jane said. "But you can cut off a hand. With his

shirt and the broken-off ax handle he made a tourniquet, and he cut his left wrist clean in two. There was a granny woman, a slave too old to work, who lived in a nearby swamp. She hid Pliny and nursed him back to health and gave him a little fishing skiff. Pliny traced his wife all the way down the river to New Orleans. That's where he met Charles II, who brought him north and had him educated."

"But he never did find his wife?" Jim said.

"No. He never did find his wife. He went back down south to look more than once. First during the Civil War, which is how he wound up in Andersonville. Again several times during Reconstruction, when he and his students were setting up schools for former slaves. But he never found her."

"Gramp never told me any of this."

"I don't think he knows, James. To the best of my knowledge, Pliny told the story of his wife, and how he lost his hand, to just one other person, a chum of mine. She swore me to secrecy for as long as she and Pliny were alive. I think they were lovers."

Jim waited for Miss Jane to tell him who that other person was, but she didn't. All she said was, "It's turning colder, James. Let us get back to work."

"Cousin Jane?"

"Aye?"

"What are we digging up here?"

"A grave, James."

Jim gestured at the figures tied to the sides of the hay wagon. "Why did you bring them?"

"To bear witness," Miss Jane said. "Now let us return to work before it comes off to snow. Our false spring is over."

Jane was right. By mid-afternoon the wind had swung around into the north and it was sharply colder. The grave, which was about twice the size of an ordinary grave, was finished. "Fetch me my father's rifle from the wagon, James."

Jim gave a start. "What for?"

"Heavens to heavens, child. Your old relation isn't going to shoot herself. Is that what you thought? I'm going to put down the horse."

"Put down the horse! There's nothing wrong with the horse."

"He's ancient, like me," Jane said. "I promised my father that I'd never let an animal leave the farm for a situation where it might be abused. If I pass on before the horse, it might fall into the hands of someone who would mistreat it. I gave my father my word. It was every bit as much a covenant as the one Pliny made with God."

After a stunned moment Jim said, "If anything happens to you, I'll take Black Hawk down to our place. I promise I will."

"You may well be off at college. Who'd care for the horse then?"

"Dad and Mom would."

"Your parents aren't spring chickens, James. They could both be dead, too."

"Jesus, Miss Jane. Black Hawk's what, twenty-five? How many more years does he have? This doesn't make sense."

"I didn't say it did. I don't know of much that makes sense, James, up here in the Kingdom or beyond. What I said was, I made a covenant with my father. I am willing to make the same covenant with you. If you will promise to me that you will shoot the horse, and bury him here next to me if I go first, then we won't need to go any further with this today."

Jim looked at Miss Jane, hoping that she might change her mind and give him a better choice. He suspected she'd planned this from the start.

"All right," he finally said. "If you go first, I'll dispose of the horse."

"Then we have a covenant," Jane said. "My people, who are also your people, have borne witness to it."

High above the mountain, a flock of geese went barking over, heading south. Jim wondered if they might be the same flock he'd heard going north the night before. Jane picked up her shovel and began refilling the grave. Jim reached for his shovel and joined her.

Later, as they walked back down the mountainside next to the horse, it started to snow, flakes of sugar snow as large as the palm of Jim's hand, the snow that came in maple sugaring season. The sugar snow was heavy and wet on Jim's face, the final sign of the upside-down weather.

Jim wondered who Jane's chum was, the girl Pliny had told his story to. Could the chum be fictitious? Could Jane and Pliny have been lovers? He doubted he'd ever know.

Jim had no intention of shooting Black Hawk if Jane died

before the horse did. If necessary, he'd make another covenant, one with his parents, to care for the horse while he was
in college. By doing so he would fail Jane and her people, his
people, who had borne witness to his promise. In his heart he
had already failed his ancestors and lied to Jane.

"What does make sense?" Jim said as they came into the
dusky barnyard. "You said not much makes sense. What
does?"

"Love," Miss Jane said. "Love and love alone makes sense.
Carry my people into the house, Jim. I'll put the horse in the
stable."

8

Territory but Little Known

The summits of Kingdom and Canada Mountains and the Great Northern Bog north of Ponds One, Two, and Three are in fact boreal fragments of the Canadian Far North. On the treeless, windswept mountaintops grow the Alpine bilberry, black crowberry, Bigelow's sedge, purple and yellow mountain saxifrages, and bird's-eye primrose. In the Great Bog one may find cotton grass, Labrador tea, and northern rosemary. In the surrounding black-spruce and cedar forest, I have sighted northern three-toed woodpeckers, lemmings, the Canada lynx, gray wolf, and both snowy and great gray owls. In all respects these last remnants of the original wilderness of "God's Kingdom" resemble the subarctic tundra a thousand miles to the north more than they do the rest of Vermont and New England.

—PLINY'S *HISTORY*

Jim and Gramp waited on the station platform. The temperature had been fifteen degrees below zero when they'd left the farmhouse. The forecast for the St. Lawrence River Valley and Laurentian Mountains of Quebec, always more accurate for the Kingdom than the forecasts for Burlington and Montpelier, called for frigid weather for the next three days.

Gramp pointed down the track with one big leather mitten. "There she is. The old Cannonball."

Far down the line Jim saw the round eye of the diesel locomotive. The light was bright in the slant winter sunshine. Jim shifted his pack basket. He loved the surge of excitement he felt when he saw a train.

The Cannonball consisted of a mail car, a baggage car used mainly for milk cans, three empty flatbeds with stake sides, the blunt-nosed locomotive, and a rust-colored caboose. Jim and Gramp rode in the caboose.

The Cannonball ran along the spur line up the east side of the big lake to Magog, Quebec. Once it passed the South Bay there was just room enough for the tracks and the single-lane dirt road beside them to squeeze between the frozen lake and the mountains.

Gramp liked to tell Jim that the Cannonball was the slowest train in North America. Its top speed was thirty-five miles an hour. Between the Common and the Great Earthen Dam at the mouth of the Upper Kingdom River it stopped half a dozen times to drop off empty milk cans on wooden scaffolds beside the tracks, where snowy lanes led back to rough-looking farms.

"This is us, Jim," Gramp said when the train stopped just south of the dam before crossing into Canada. "To quote a certain newspaper editor well-known to us both, let's get this show on the road. Don't forget your pack basket."

. . .

It was three miles up the frozen Dead Water impoundment under the cliffs in the notch between Kingdom and Canada Mountains, then another mile along the rapids, which never froze, to Pond Number Three and the hunting camp, where Jim and Gramp would spend the weekend. Even though he no longer hunted deer, Jim still loved to go to camp. This weekend was special because Jim would have Gramp and his stories to himself.

As they started up the impoundment on the snowshoes Gramp had made with white-ash frames and deer-hide thongs, Jim carried the pack basket containing their food, ice-fishing tip-ups, shotguns, and extra clothing. Gramp went first. At seventy-six, he moved over the snow swiftly and easily. Overhead, the ice on the rock walls of Kingdom and Canada Mountains was every shade of blue and green. The ice walls were a thousand feet high. Once Jim had asked Gramp if anyone could climb them. Gramp had looked up at the cliffs. "A man can do what he has to," he'd said. Jim was glad he didn't have to climb the cliffs.

One day when Jim and Gramp were fishing the impoundment in a late-summer drought, they had looked far down into the water and seen, wavering in the pulse of the Dead Water, the blackened church steeple and burned-out stone houses of New Canaan. Today the ice was a foot thick, but thinking about the incinerated village below his snowshoes made the bottoms of Jim's feet tingle.

Gramp came to a sudden stop. He pointed across the ice,

where a spring open year-round spilled straight down the rock wall of Canada Mountain into a pocket of ice-free water three or four feet in diameter beside the bottom of the cliff. Humping its way along the ice toward the spring hole was a river otter. It stood up on its short hind legs and looked at Gramp and Jim. Then it slipped into the open water and vanished under the ice. A minute passed. Another. Jim's breath began to come tighter. What if the otter couldn't find the hole again? It would be trapped below the ice.

The otter popped up, slid out onto the ice, and undulated its way toward a stand of hemlock trees at the foot of the mountain. In its jaws was a brook trout a good sixteen inches long. Gramp grinned at Jim, who grinned back. It was a fine sight to see a river otter catch a trout. It was better yet to see such a sight together.

They heard the rapids before they saw them, then spotted the steam rising above the rushing water, pink in the reflected rays of the sunset. They snowshoed up the game trail inside the dusky cedars beside the rapids. Twenty minutes later they came out a few hundred yards downriver from the old driving dam at the outlet of Three. There was the camp, on the hardwood slope above the dam. In the noiseless winter twilight, with no smoke curling out of the stovepipe jutting through the roof, the camp looked like a painting of itself.

While Gramp got a fire going in the Glenwood, Jim shoveled a path up to the camp door from the pond and another from the door to the privy. In places the drifts were waist-deep. Jim used the camp ax to hack a hole through the ice on the pond. He carried two pails of water up to the camp, one for drinking and one for washing. Before leaving camp the past fall, Jim had packed the woodbox full of sugar-maple, yellow-birch, and ash splits.

The Glenwood was beginning to throw heat. Gramp had lighted the kerosene lamps on the table and the shelf above his old-man's rocking chair. He seared the camp skillet and slapped in a quarter pound of salted butter from Mom's Ruthie cow and tossed in a two-pound slab of beefsteak. He'd already peeled two of Mom's Green Mountain potatoes and set them to boil. Along with the steak and potatoes, Mom had sent up butternut squash, already cooked and ready to warm up, and an apple pie from the Westfield Seek-No-Further tree in the dooryard; also a cooked roast chicken from her flock of leghorns for tomorrow in case the partridge hunting was slow.

Before setting the table with the heavy, off-white camp crockery and mismatched flatware, Jim made the entry for the day in the ledger:

Jan. 20, 1955. Rode local to dam with Gramp, snowshoed up still water to God's Kingdom. Saw an otter take a trout, 1½–2 pounds, out of spring hole at base of Canada Mountain. Temperature at 6:00 P.M. 25° below. Twenty inches of ice on Three. James Kinneson III.

After supper Gramp sat beside the stove in his rocker, sipping from a tumbler of blackberry brandy. Gramp never drank except at camp. There he'd sip one glass of his own brandy, made from the long blackberries that grew on the slope above the barn on the farm that wasn't. Gramp said that his blackberry toddy at camp was to fortify his heart for the next day's hunt.

"I didn't know there was anything wrong with your heart," Jim teased him.

"That's because when I come up here I fortify it," Gramp said. "It's a family tradition."

Jim, sitting at the cleared table, looking through the camp journal, waited for the story he was sure would follow. He didn't know what the tale would be. Only that there would be one.

"What I mean by 'family tradition,'" Gramp said, "is that the only place my father and Pliny drank was here at God's Kingdom. Pliny being a clergyman, and a Presbyterian clergyman at that, was expected never to let a drop pass his lips. It would have cost him his jobs, as minister and as headmaster. My dad was all but a teetotaler himself. The great irony being that he, and his father and his, all staunch Presbyterian deacons, operated the largest whiskey distillery in New England. True, they used every penny of their very considerable profits to finance their abolitionist activities. The *Monitor* and the farm were mutual drains on each other, but as destitute as they were from time to time, the Kinnesons never used a penny of income from the distillery for any of their personal expenses. Or touched a dram of the stuff themselves anyplace but here at camp."

"I'm surprised they drank here knowing how straitlaced those old Presbyterians were."

Gramp sipped his brandy. "Oh, they didn't actually drink

anyplace—even, here—son. They just 'tasted.' They'd bring
three or four stone bottles from the aging warehouse up here
to sample and see if it was ready to sell. 'Will you have a taste,
brother? Just a sup to see how it progresses?' 'Aye, brother, I
don't know but what I will. Just a sup.' They'd have their sups
and then one of them might say, 'Not quite, I think.' The
other one would nod, and they'd look quite sorrowfully at the
stone bottle on the table. Then, very solemnly, my father or
Pliny would say, 'Well, a toast. To universal emancipation.'
'To universal emancipation, brother.' Over the course of the
evening those two old devils would taste and sample and sup
and toast their way through two or three quart stone bottles
and then walk over to their bunks as gravely and deliberately
as two tipsy geese."

Jim laughed. For a time, as Jim paged through the camp
journal, neither he nor Gramp spoke. Then Jim said, "Listen
to this."

> *June 16, 1868. Caught 17 trout, 12–18 inches, on Green
> Drake fished dry on Ponds One and Two. P. Templeton.*
>
> *June 17, 1868. Caught 19 trout, 15–19 inches, on Royal
> Coachman lead fly, Silver Doctor and Queen of the
> Waters dropper flies, fished wet. Charles Kinneson II.*

Jim said, "It's almost as if Pliny and your father were competing with each other over who could catch the most and biggest trout."

"They were," Gramp said. "Competing with each other.
There was always a pretty brisk rivalry between them for, I

don't know, call it moral ascendancy. Moral in the broadest sense, I mean. If one of them made a garden a hundred feet long by fifty feet wide, the other would immediately spade up a plot one hundred and fifty feet long by seventy-five feet wide. Dr. T, as we schoolkids called him, didn't hunt. I don't imagine that hunting held much allure for someone who'd been hunted himself. When it came to angling, though, you can see for yourself from the camp ledger. He and my father spent entire days up here vying to outfish each other.

"My father never did play baseball. He was just that much older than Pliny, fifteen years, that he never learned. In fact, I think he was a little disdainful of the game. Hidebound old Highlander that he was, he couldn't see the utility of it. Or the utility of any game, for that matter. Also, as a Presbyterian born and bred, Father seemed to be suspicious of any pursuit that smacked of fun for its own sake.

"Both men, of course, were strong Lincoln Republicans and abolitionists. They agreed on that much. Religion was a different story, and of the two of them, my father was much more of a doctrinaire. Pliny was no freethinker, far from it, but he prided himself on never criticizing anyone for their faith or lack thereof, except himself."

"He must have been a good minister," Jim said.

Gramp nodded. "He was. But he was an even better teacher. He could teach anybody anything, Jimmy. Solid geometry, English composition, botany. You name it, Dr. T could teach it. Also, he made sure we could find north, and tell the names of the planets and constellations. In the summertime, he taught us how to swim, if we didn't already know how, in the catch basin below the High Falls. And how to cook. He told us a good cook, man or woman, would never be out of a job. He taught us boys to box and he taught us and the girls, as well, to play baseball, and played right alongside of us.

"Best of all, Jim, he was a born storyteller. We pupils used to beg for certain favorites in order to derail him from the lesson of the day. 'Getting Old Temp going,' we called it. 'Tell us how you arm wrestled John Brown for a chance to work on the Underground Railroad, Dr. T. Tell how you picked up Charles Kinneson's sword and helped beat back Pickett's charge at Gettysburg with it. And how you escaped from Andersonville.'

"*Crack!* Down would come his schoolmastering cane, Jack Regulator, on the edge of the teacher's dais. 'I'll tell you to get out your McGuffeys, miscreants, and be quick about it. Otherwise, you'll have a taste of Jack.' 'Old Dr. Bluster,' we called him, behind his back. He never did have the heart to cane us. And yes, sooner rather than later he'd tell us his wonderful old stories. We'd gotten Old Temp going again."

"But he never did tell you about his life as a slave, before coming north?" Jim said.

"Nope," Gramp said. "He never did. It was as if his life didn't begin until the day he stepped across the Mason-Dixon Line."

Gramp finished his brandy. "Well," he said. "If we're going to accomplish anything tomorrow, we'd best hit the hay tonight."

Jim filled the firebox in the Glenwood and shut down the stovepipe draft for the night. Then he went up to the loft.

Gramp blew out the wicks in the kerosene lamps and made his way across the uneven floor of the camp to his bunk. A few minutes later they were both asleep.

The next day was colder yet. The thermometer on the privy door read forty-two below zero. For breakfast Gramp fried eggs in the grease left over from last night's steak, cut up home fries, and made buckwheat cakes laced with maple syrup. They drank camp coffee, and topped off with stewed prunes from the Canada plum tree behind the farmhouse. After breakfast Jim did the dishes while Gramp tidied up the camp and scattered bread crumbs on the snow outside for the chickadees.

"It's warmed up to thirty," Gramp said. "Thirty below, that is. I call that good winter weather, Jim. Let's go scout up some grouse for a game supper tonight."

They headed up the slope behind the camp on their snowshoes, climbing side by side through the leafless hardwoods, moving slowly so they wouldn't sweat and then take a chill. A large, dark bird flushed from below a sugar maple tree. Jim started to raise his shotgun, then saw the flash of red on the bird's head. It was a pileated woodpecker, the bird Gramp called Lord God because of its regal crimson cockade. Gramp pointed at the base of the maple tree, where the woodpecker had hammered out an oblong cavity a foot high and several inches wide, searching for insects that bored their way into the tree. A heap of fresh wood chips lay on the snow.

"It's good luck to see a Lord God bird, Jim."

"Why?"

"It means the woods are healthy. If somebody waltzes in here and clear-cuts the mountainside, the pileated woodpeckers are going to pack their bags and move north to Canada."

Jim gestured across the river. "At least they won't have far to go."

A few minutes later Gramp shot a grouse out of a popple tree it was budding. Another one rocketed out of the deep snow ahead. Jim hurried his shot and missed. A few minutes later he got two grouse budding a yellow birch.

Halfway up the mountainside they crossed the faint trace through the trees, now mostly grown up, where the Canada Post Road had once run up to the border. Gramp chuckled. "A good many loads of Canadian booze traveled along this old woods road during Prohibition, Jim. I was all for the smugglers. It was Prohibition that finally did in the family distillery. The runners would bring booze into Vermont on the train sometimes, too, in milk cans or hidden under pulpwood or logs. And a lot of it came down the lake by motor launch."

Jim loved hunting up the mountain with Gramp at this time of the year. In the summer the leaves were too thick for them to see much. Climbing the mountain with Gramp in the winter when you could see off to the south and east for miles was like traveling back into history.

From the Balancing Boulder on top of the mountain, high above the tree line, he and Gramp could look out 360 degrees, at the entire Kingdom. Far below on the frozen Dead Water a black dot was inching its way across the ice.

"Bog lemming," Gramp said. "I haven't seen more than three or four in my life."

Suddenly Gramp pointed at the cliff face of Canada Mountain, across the notch.

A very large white bird had launched itself off a ledge and was plummeting, wings folded, toward the frozen impoundment below. At the last moment it leveled out of its free fall and swooped up the lemming in its talons, then swiftly ascended to its ledge a thousand feet above the ice.

"Great Snowy?" Jim said.

"Gyrfalcon," Gramp said. "Right down from the tundra. It must be a very tough winter up north, Jim. I don't know anyone else who's ever seen one here in the Kingdom."

Jim grinned. "Is it good luck? To see one?"

"Not for the lemming it wasn't," Gramp said. "Let's head back to camp before we freeze solid up here. I wouldn't be surprised if the temperature hits fifty below tonight."

On the way down the mountain Gramp shot a snowshoe hare turned white for winter. Back at the camp Jim dressed out the partridges and hare, careful not to slice into the rabbit's gallbladder and spoil the meat. Then he cut half a dozen holes in the ice on Three. Gramp brought down the tip-ups in a pail and baited their hooks with strips of pork rind. Almost immediately one of the red-cloth flags snapped up and Jim reeled in a thrashing foot-long brook trout. In less than an hour they had six trout from twelve to about fifteen inches. In the winter months the bellies of the fish were pale, but their backs were a beautiful forest green and their sides were sprinkled with red speckles ringed with powdery-blue halos. Inside, the winter trout were as orange as salmon.

"I didn't know there was an ice-fishing season for brookies," Jim said. "What's the limit?"

"How many can you eat?" Gramp said. "That's the limit."

While Jim refilled the woodbox, Gramp peeled and cut up into the game stew four more of Mom's big potatoes, half a dozen carrots, several onions, and a yellow turnip. He fried the brook trout in butter in the camp skillet and they feasted on rabbit-and-partridge stew and freshly caught trout and Mom's homemade bread warmed in the overhead warming oven of the Glenwood. For dessert they split one of Mom's maple-sugar pies.

Jim heated water on the stove and did the dishes. Gramp made the day's entry in the camp ledger. "Be sure to mention the gyrfalcon," Jim said.

"You think I'd forget to do that?" Gramp said. "Pliny Templeton was pretty sure they came down here once in a great while. He wanted in the worst way to see one for his *History*."

Gramp closed the ledger. "What do you know about the trouble in the family, Jim?"

Jim turned quickly away from the wooden sink, the damp dish towel still in his hand, to face Gramp. In that era in God's Kingdom, certain family secrets—suicides, children born out of wedlock, mental illnesses—were rarely discussed.

"I know Charles II, your father, shot Pliny. That's how

Pliny's skeleton got the two holes in its skull. Pliny wanted to introduce a music program at the Academy. Your dad, being a strict old-school Presbyterian, and president of the school board, opposed the idea. Pliny brought in a piano and that was the final straw."

Gramp nodded. "That's the gist of it. My father went right off the deep end and murdered his best friend and adoptive brother. He spent the last years of his life chained to his bed at the state insane asylum. I was in my third year at the university when the murder took place. I had to drop out of school and come home to run the paper and the distillery and the farm. It was a terrible stain on the family. We've never really lived it down. I've tried to shield your dad from it, and you and Charlie, too, by not talking about it. Lately, I've come to think that was a mistake. It happened. It happened and you, especially, need to know as much about it as I can tell you."

Gramp pointed at his rocker. "Sit down, Jim."

"I don't want to take your chair," Jim said.

"Go ahead. That'll be your chair someday."

Jim sat down in Gramp's chair. Then Gramp began his story. "After my older sister, Mary, went to live in New Canaan with the stonecutters, and then died with everyone else in the Great Fire of '82, my father was said never to be the same. He kept the distillery going—by then the proceeds were paying for the schools Pliny was setting up in the South for emancipated Negroes—and the newspaper. He editorialized tirelessly against the so-called wars with the western Indians, and against the Spanish-American War. He said we had every bit as much right to claim the Philippine Islands as we did the

moon and the sun. And he was never anything less than a kind
and even indulgent father to me. My father continued to be ac-
tive in the governance of the church and school and to hunt
and fish. But as I came into my teens I could see him chang-
ing. He'd run on for hours about riding with John Brown at
Harper's Ferry. I believe he felt somehow guilty about getting
away scot-free and leaving Brown to his fate there. And he'd
hash over Pickett's charge, and his and Pliny's imprisonment
at Andersonville, and Charles I's massacring those Abenaki
fishers, and the federal troops annihilating his father James I's
ragtag little band of secessionists. More and more my father
had the look of a haunted man.

"The trouble took place in the summer of 1900. That was
the year they built the Great Earthen Dam at the mouth of the
Upper Kingdom and flooded out the remains of New Canaan.
I think that brought back to my father the fire and the deaths
of my sister and nearly a hundred former slaves and their families. He editorialized against the dam, too. He accused its
backers of wanting to put the people of New Canaan out of
sight, out of mind. Above all, he editorialized against the Ku
Klux Klan."

"The Klan? The same Klan that lynched Negroes down
south?"

"Yes," Gramp said. "And they didn't just murder Negroes
down south, Jim. They murdered Negroes up north, too.
Who did you suppose burned out New Canaan?"

"I thought New Canaan burned in the Great Forest Fire of
'82."

"It was the other way around. The Klan came riding up

the old Canada Post Road in their white sheets and hoods and caught the villagers at Sunday evening services inside the church. They barred the door and hurled Greek fire in sealed glass jars through the windows. A volatile paste of sulfur and phosphorous that burst into white-hot flames on contact with the air. There'd been a bad drought and the woods were tinder dry. The burning village acted like a fuse, setting the forest on fire."

"I never knew that," Jim said. He felt physically sick to think of the people, including Gramp's sister, trapped inside the burning church.

"Well, there's more," Gramp said. "Soon after the Great Forest Fire, the Klansmen who had fired New Canaan began boasting about what they'd done. Once word of their identity got out, an avenging specter, arrayed in a black cape and astride a pale horse shod in black crepe, would appear, as if from nowhere, in the dooryard of a Klansman and call him out by name. Some of the Klansmen, I'm sorry to say, were our own shirttail relatives. 'You, Nathan Bedford Kinneson!' the apparition on horseback would roar out. 'A word with you, sir.' Some he shot down with a great long horse pistol. Others he hacked to pieces with the sword John Brown had given him. There was no escape from him.

"One evening—I would have been six or at most seven at the time—as I was shooing the chickens into the henhouse for the night, I heard angry voices coming from the barn. I slipped into the haymow and peered down the chute into the stable, where the voices were coming from. There below, I made out my father and Pliny Templeton and Father's riding horse. Father was kneeling beside the horse, doing something by lantern light with a bucket and a brush. At first I couldn't imagine what he was up to. Then I realized that he was white-washing it. The horse didn't like it. Every several seconds he'd stamp one of his hind feet. But he was a very tractable animal, and like Father and Pliny, a veteran of the war, so he stood there and allowed himself to be painted. Father was dressed in a black cape and he was wearing his sword.

" 'Aye, brother,' my father was saying. 'You have smoked me out. Your assumption is correct. Surely you, who know me as well as any true brother ever knew his brother, did not suppose that I would permit the murderers of our New Canaanite brethren and my beloved daughter to go unpunished?'

" 'Brother!' Pliny cried out. 'I implore you. Vengeance belongs to the Lord.'

" 'True. And I am His instrument.'

" 'You are no such thing! You endanger your immortal soul.'

"My father stood up, and fell to whitewashing the horse's back. Then, in a lower voice, almost as though he was speaking to himself, he repeated, 'I am His appointed instrument, as Brown was before me.'

"At the time, Jim, I was too young to understand exactly what I was witnessing. I didn't know about the killing of the Klansmen in their own barnyards, only that Father and Dr. Templeton, who was already like an uncle to me, were genuinely angry with each other. I retreated from my spying perch and ran out of the mow, crying. That in itself was unusual. Children didn't cry much in those days. But I bawled like a bull-calf taken from its mother. Did my own mother know what my father was doing? I don't know. Did the Common suspect who was behind the killing of the Klansmen? Very likely it did. Not much happens in a village that it doesn't know about. I was twelve or thirteen before I fully understood what I'd seen that night, and I never told anyone. So far as I know, Pliny and my father didn't discuss the matter again. No doubt they each had their secrets, and it isn't the way of country people to hash over past deeds that can't be undone. Once I heard my father ask Pliny if he believed that the sins of the father were visited on their sons. Pliny said no, but I doubt Father was referring to himself and his descendants. I doubt he ever regarded killing the Klansmen as a sin. There were nineteen in all. Nineteen shot or hacked to pieces or both. Who knows if they'd all ridden on New Canaan? Some were scarcely out of their boyhood."

Gramp got up, slipped into his mackinaw, and headed out to the privy. A couple of minutes later he called Jim outside to see the northern lights. The aurora came and went in vivid electric colors, shooting high into the sky to the north. "God's fireworks," Gramp said. "That's what Pliny calls them in his *History*. God's fireworks."

And later, in their bunks, "There's something about what you told me, Gramp. Something I don't understand."

"There are fifty somethings about what I told you that I don't understand. What is it?"

"You said I, especially, needed to know as much about Pliny's murder as you could tell me. Why me especially?"

"So you can write about it."

"Why don't you write about it?"

"That's not the kind of writer I am, Jim. You're the story-teller in the family. I'm a newspaperman. I can't make any-thing up. Or leave anything out. From the time you could spell *cat* you were inventing stories."

Jim thought about what Gramp had said. Then he said, "Which is more important? Being able to make things up or being able to leave things out?"

"Inventing. If you can't make things up, there's no story. But leaving things out is pretty important, too. If you can't leave things out, nobody'll read what you write."

"Can I ask you one more question?"

"You can ask me one hundred questions. There's no guar-antee I can answer any of them."

"If I make some things up and leave other things out, then they won't be true stories."

"Sure they will. They'll be your true stories. The stories I tell you are your legacy. What you do with them is up to you. It's all still territory but little known. Waiting for you to ex-plore it. Let's grab a few hours of sleep, son. Morning comes early up here in God's Kingdom."

9

The Scout

*Someone, perhaps Samuel Clemens, said that every story be-
gins with a stranger coming to town or with a man or a woman
going on a journey. Certainly this definition holds true for most
of the best stories of God's Kingdom, from the arrival of Charles
Kinneson I onward.*

—PLINY'S *HISTORY*

He wore a too-large suit jacket with a herringbone pattern, worn at the elbows; black dress shoes; dark slacks
frayed at the cuffs; a white shirt yellowing around the collar;
and a broad black necktie. He had a sharp-featured face and
carried a carpetbag. He was clean-shaven, of medium build.
He looked about fifty. His hair was still quite dark and neatly
parted. His eyes were gray and quiet, and in their still attentive-
ness when they alighted on you, you could feel him thinking.

"Looking for this, I presume?" the stranger said, holding
out a grass-stained baseball. The Outlaws, who'd taken their
old name back because no one knew who the White Knights
were, had been practicing on the common when Charlie

swatted a foul ball over the backstop and across the street off the roof of the railroad station. As the team's youngest player, Jim had been dispatched to retrieve it.

The stranger on the railway platform flipped Jim the ball. Jim guessed that he'd probably come into town on the 6:16 northbound, now whistling at the River Road crossing. The stranger cocked his head like a bird listening for a worm. Then he said, "Young man, I am no prognosticator. Neither in my view is any other human man or woman. Like you say, the future is as blank as your scorecard before you pencil in the lineup. But if you can tell me how far off that train whistle is, I might be able to tell you if your ball game is going to be washed out."

"A mile and a half," Jim said. "But it isn't a game. Just practice."

"Practice won't hurt," the stranger said. "Baseball is a game of inches and a game of luck. The more you practice, the luckier you get."

The stranger spoke in an accent Jim thought might be southern. He wet the tip of his forefinger and held it up to the breeze. "Wind outen the north," he said as the whistle hooted again. "Fluty sounding but plain enough. Air's kindly heavy this evening. So you tell me. Is it fixing to rain?"

Jim shrugged. "I don't know."

"No one knows, son. Weather? Baseball? Will it be heaven or will it be hell? Nobody can tell the future and that's a natural fact. But if it's a traveling train whistle to judge by, or even if it isn't, you'll never go wrong to say, 'It always has.' Rained, that is."

The stranger put out his hand. "Most call me the Scout. On account of that would be what I am."

"Jim Kinneson," Jim said, shaking hands. "Scout as in baseball scout?"

The stranger looked Jim up and down with his assessing eyes. "Shortstop?"

Jim nodded.

"Leadoff hitter? Pick 'em up and put 'em down on the base path, can you?"

Jim nodded again.

"Who's your big-league club up here? Who do you go for?"

"The Red Sox," Jim said.

"My condolences to you," the Scout said. He set his carpet-bag on the bench outside the station. He rummaged in the satchel, then pulled out a baseball cap with a bright red bird above the bill. He put it back in the bag and got out a cap embossed with a feather, then one with the letters NY entwined on it. Hurriedly, he thrust the NY cap back in his grip. Finally he located a blue cap with an ornate red B piped out in white. Just as he put it on, the train whistle gave one last wail.

"Let's play ball, Mr. Leadoff Hitter Shortstop," he said, picking up his bag. "We got us an hour at the outside before the deluge hits."

The Scout sat on the top row of the empty bleachers on the first-base side of the diamond. The Outlaws looked at him curiously. Jim swung two bats in the on-deck circle while Charlie finished taking his rips. "Who's your bud in the Sox cap?" Charlie said.

"He's a baseball scout," Jim said.

"Is that so? Harley," Charlie called out to the pitcher. "Lob me two, three more."

Harlan Kittredge floated in a pitch that might have broken a pane of glass. Charlie popped it sky-high between first and second. "That ought to bring on the rain," the Scout said to no one in particular.

Little Ti Thibideau, the team's forty-year-old water boy, gave a whoop. He pointed at Charlie. "Hey, b-b-b-batter. Hey, batter, batter, b-b-b-batter."

Charlie leveled his bat belt-high across the plate. "Right here, Harley K."

Harlan went into an exaggerated windup and flipped one down the pike over the heart of the plate. Charlie caught all of it and drove the ball high off the bandstand in deep center field, a good four hundred feet away.

"Hell damn!" Little Ti said. "That's a home run in any m-m-major-league ballpark."

"As long as you s-s-say so, Ti," Harlan said.

The boys laughed. The Scout was writing in a pocket memorandum book with the nub of a pencil. Jim wasn't sure he'd even seen Charlie's blast.

"Okay, bub, show 'em what you've got," Charlie said as Jim stepped into the batter's box.

With the Scout watching, Jim was nervous at first. He got out on his front foot too soon and topped a weak comebacker to Harlan. "Hey, batter, batter, b-b-b-batter," Ti chanted.

Soon Jim found his rhythm. His swings were compact and crisp and the ball seemed to jump off his bat. He drove one pitch after another exactly where it was pitched. In the hole between short and third, up the middle over second. Into the gaps in the outfield.

"Okay, Jimbo, lay one down and hoof it out," Harlan said. Jim dropped a bunt down the third-base line and sprinted to first. At sixteen he was the fastest player on the team.

"Wait till you see him throw some leather out at short," Charlie called up to the Scout. The Scout winced as if he'd pulled something in his back.

Jim walked over to the bleachers to get his glove. "Well?" he said.

"Well, what?" the Scout said.

"Did you see anything?"

"I saw you look back over your shoulder when you were dogging it down to first. Don't do that."

Jim grinned. "Something might be gaining, right?"

"Not in this backwater it won't be," the Scout said. "It's nothing up here to gain. Looking back slows you down a step. What does that billboard say?"

"What billboard?"

"Over yonder." The Scout jerked his thumb over his shoulder. "Up top the factory roof. I can't make it out without my eyeglasses."

"It says '81 Days Without an Accident,'" Jim said. He noticed that the Scout was wearing his glasses.

"What was the last one?"

Jim thought. "Lefty Greene, our number two pitcher, got his shirtsleeve caught in the planer. He lost his arm."

"Right or left?"

"Left."

"Yes, sir," the Scout said. "Know anyone who works there?"

"Half the guys on the team work there. I'm working there this summer."

"Big fella with the mouth on him. Hit just before you did. He work there?"

"That's my brother, Charlie. No, he's an attorney. All Ivy League catcher out of Dartmouth. First in his class at Harvard Law School."

The Scout stood up. "Is there a hotel in this burg?"

Jim pointed up the green at the Common Hotel, across the street from the bandstand.

"Eatery?"

"On the ground floor of the hotel."

The Scout picked up his carpetbag. He peered at the cloudless sky. The storm had blown over without raining a drop. "Didn't I tell you?"

"Tell me what?" Jim said.

"That no man can predict the weather. Meet me at that hotel eatery at six sharp, Jim. Bring your Ivy League brother."

Jim and Charlie were ten minutes early. The Scout was waiting for them at the window table overlooking the common. As they came into the dining room, he took out a round dollar watch and frowned at it as if they were late.

"You boys don't own neckties?"

Charlie laughed. "Up here in the Kingdom we don't usually dress for dinner. This isn't the Waldorf Astoria."

"I'll give you that," the Scout said, looking around at the trophy deer heads and trout mounted on the dining room walls. "But Waldorf Astoria or East Overshoe, Vermont, if a man is wearing a necktie and his shoes are polished, I call that man properly dressed. Sit down, boys. My dime tonight."

"So," Charlie said. "How many have you signed up this summer?"

"Nary a one," the Scout said. "Mainly, the prospects turn out to be a lot of hot air. When the time comes to set down their John Henry, they get cold feet."

This didn't make sense to Jim. He'd give his eyeteeth to be signed to a contract. So would Charlie or any of the other Outlaws.

Armand St. Onge came over to the table to take their orders. All three ordered steak sandwiches and fries. Charlie ordered a cold one from the bar. After Armand brought him his beer, Charlie said, "I don't understand. Why would your prospects get cold feet?"

"Timid," the Scout said. "Afraid the owners will pick up stakes and pull out."

For a moment he regarded Jim and Charlie with his still gray eyes. Then he said, "A. J. Peabody, gentlemen. Advance man for the United Woodworkers of America, out of Peoria,

Illinois. Do a little baseball scouting on the side. Let's get to work."

Jim's father once told him that the village of Kingdom Common was as close to a company town as it could come without actually being one. The American Furniture factory—or, as it was universally called in the Kingdom, the mill—sprawled out along the railroad tracks beside the Lower Kingdom River. The blowers on its roof could be heard night and day from every corner of the village, often punctuated by the clashing together of boxcars, the rumbling of the yard locomotive, and the *slam-bang* of boards being stacked in the lumberyard. Morning, noon, and at five o'clock in the afternoon, the mill whistle regulated the comings and goings of the workers. Six days a week the village was suffused with the scents of varnish and shellac. Before Jim's time the mill had paid its workers not in cash but in scrip, redeemable only at the company store. Mr. Arthur Anderson, whose grandfather had established the American factory, still rented out apartments to mill workers in the row of battleship-gray wooden tenements along the river known locally as the beehives.

Working at the mill during the summer before his senior year at the Academy had not been Jim's idea. He'd hoped to write for the *Monitor* full-time. Instead, his dad had insisted that he apply at the factory, which provided seasonal employment for high-school and college kids. Some years ago, when Charlie was Jim's age, their father had made him take a summer job at the mill. Jim suspected that the editor wanted his sons to know what a hellhole the place was as an incentive to tend to their studies and go on to college. At best, a job at the mill was a dusty, loud, low-paying stop on the way to somewhere, almost anywhere, else. For Jim, and for Charlie before him, it was a cautionary taste of experience in the real world. For many of its workers it was a trap from which there was no escape.

At the mill, as Jim had quickly learned, there was an unspoken caste system. At the top was Mr. Anderson. Once a week, usually on Monday morning, he would walk through the entire factory like a captain inspecting his ship. Mr. Anderson was in his mid-eighties and a little stiff and tottery, but he walked as straight as a palace guard and spoke courteously by name to each worker. Charlie had remarked to Jim that old Arthur Anderson was a benevolent despot, but a despot all the same.

Directly below the owner on the factory hierarchy was Bennett Carol, the superintendent, who had worked at the mill for fifty years. Then, in descending rank, came the foremen of the mill floor, cabinet room, finish room, and lumberyard; the master cabinetmakers who assembled the furniture; the machine operators; and the men who tailed the machines, stacked lumber, and packed the finished furniture and loaded it onto boxcars.

At the bottom of the ladder were the seasonal helpers, like Jim, who did certain repetitive but necessary jobs no one else coveted. In the eyes of the foremen and workers alike, Jim and the other temporary help at the factory had no status at all.

On the morning after he and Charlie had met with A. J.

Peabody at the hotel, Jim began work, as usual, by climbing up the inside metal ladder to the trapdoor leading to the roof to update the accident-free message board. Today was Day 82. Then he reported to Bennett Carol for his work assignment.

"Day 82," as the workers would now refer to it, was a Saturday. On Saturdays the mill closed for the weekend at noon. Jim hoped he'd be assigned to spend the rest of the morning working for Ned Baxter in the lumberyard. He loved the fresh scent of boards curing in the open air, and Ned was a good man to work for. From him, Jim had learned how to identify black cherry, maple, yellow-birch, and white-pine lumber. He'd learned that a load of one-inch hardwood boards, after being seasoned outdoors in the yard for six months, would be dried in the kiln at 150 degrees Fahrenheit for ninety-six hours. Ned had taught him how to measure board feet in logs with a Doyle rule and in lumber with a Stanley rule. Now in his late seventies, Ned still worked alongside his crew, not fast, not slowly, but steadily, and they willingly followed his lead. He was by far the best foreman to be assigned to, but today Bennett Carol dispatched Jim to the mill floor to run the barrow. Running the barrow consisted of pushing a boxy old wheelbarrow along the mill floor, sweeping the scrap pieces of wood from the saws and other machines into it. When the barrow was full, Jim would trundle it down to the boiler room and empty the contents into the factory furnace that heated the water for the gigantic Corliss steam engine that powered the mill machinery. American Furniture was one of the last steam-powered factories in New England.

The mill-floor foreman, Rip Kinneson, a distant cousin of

Jim's, was one of the very few villagers Jim strongly disliked. He was a competent ripsawer and foreman, though he tended to hurry his work and had the reputation of a hard horse driver. His motto was "Keep moving."

No one could accuse Rip Kinneson of ever standing still. As if in testimony to his philosophy, he was missing three fingers from his right hand, the result of hurrying on his own saw. He drank a fifth of 7 Crown at the hotel every night of the week. Two shots into the evening he'd begin to complain about the two great nemeses of his life, the government and his four ex-wives. Sometimes he'd get them confused and inveigh bitterly about the exorbitant taxes he had to pay his wives and the day he married his third government. At work there was nothing amusing about him. He had an unflattering nickname for everyone. He called Mr. Anderson "the Old Man" behind his back. Jim he called Jack because he was a jack of all trades at the factory but most definitely master of none. Jim detested the name.

In good weather the workers often took their dinner pails outside and ate lunch beside the river. During their nooning the Ripper, as he referred to himself, loved to tell war stories. His favorite was a detailed account of "putting the flame-thrower to a nest of Japs holed up in a tunnel" during the fighting in the Pacific Islands. "Do you know what fricasseed Japanese smells like, Jack?"

Jim didn't and neither, Charlie assured him, did Rip. While Charlie acknowledged that the Ripper would have dearly loved to put the flamethrower to the Japanese, the closest the mill-floor foreman had ever been to the Pacific Islands was the docks at San Diego, where he'd spent his tour of duty loading navy supply ships.

Early in Jim's boyhood, his mother, Ruth Kinneson, had impressed upon him that Jesus taught us that it's always wrong to hate anyone for any reason. Jim figured that Jesus had never met the Ripper. It was widely believed in the Common that Mr. Anderson kept Rip on at the factory because as long as the mill-floor foreman was there to despise, the workers would be less apt to resent him. Rip's favorite victim was Little Ti Thibideau, the Outlaws' water boy.

"You hear the news, Ti? President Eisenhower's coming to inspect the mill this forenoon. He's going to present you with a Medal of Honor."

Or "Hey, there, Tippytoe. Have you seen today's paper? The Sox have traded Ted Williams to New York for Joe DiMaggio."

Ti never knew whether to believe Rip. "Oh, you g-g-guys," he'd say. "You, you, you guys."

Once or twice a month Rip would snatch off Ti's cap and toss it into the nearest blower pipe to be carried down to the furnace along with the sawdust from the machinery. Then Ti would stomp around and threaten to bring in the union— which union, he never specified. About ten years ago, a mill-workers' union from Maine tried to organize the employees at the factory, but nothing ever came of their effort. Rip told the men that if they voted in a union, Old Man Anderson would unbolt the woodworking machines; load them onto boxcars for South Carolina, where there was a raft of black niggers eager to work for sixty cents an hour; and lock the

doors of the factory in Kingdom Common forever. The workers had voted down the union by a two-to-one margin.

Just where Ti fit into the caste system of the mill was unclear to Jim. At the same time that he was bullied mercilessly,
Ti was respected for his unusual skill as a fixer. When a table,
a chair, or another piece of furniture came off the line flawed
or damaged—with a ding on a visible surface, say, or a leg half
an inch too short or too long—Ti could repair it so that not
even the most highly trained woodworker would notice the
imperfection. With a dab of wood glue or filler, a block plane, a
square of sandpaper no larger than a folded pocket handker-
chief, and a touch of varnish or shellac, Ti was a wizard. He
saved the factory thousands of dollars a year by restoring furniture that would otherwise have had to be sold as seconds.
More than his fundamental good nature or comical rages or
any rough sympathy inspired by his stuttering, it was Théophile Thibideau's unquestionable skill on the finish-room floor
that secured his acceptance, for all of the taunting, as one of
the guys.

At ten o'clock break time of Day 82, Rip shut off his saw
and told Jim he wanted a word with him outside where men
gathered for a quick smoke. "Listen, Jack," Rip said. "Since he
come to work this morning, Little Ti's been talking a shitload
of big talk about a union waltzing in. Telling everybody who'll
listen he's going to fix Anderson's wagon once and for all. He
says that so-called baseball scout you and brother, Charlie,
was sucking up to at the hotel last evening is a union organizer.
What do you know about all this?"

Jim's heart fell. After finishing their steak sandwiches the evening before, Jim and Charlie had introduced A. J. Peabody to half a dozen union supporters from the mill. Jim should have known that in a small town like the Common, which was no more nor less than a beehive itself, word of their conversations would leak out. He doubted that there was a worker at the factory who didn't know the scout's true identity by now.

Jim wasn't sure what to say to Rip. It was hard for him to believe that he could be related to this man. While Jim considered whether and how to reply, Rip stepped up close enough to his face for Jim to smell the liquor he'd drunk the night before. "Do you know what we do to commonist agitators up here, Jack?"

"No."

"They disappear. What would Dad Kinneson say if he knew you were keeping company with a commie agitator? Fella who comes into town pretending to be somebody he isn't?"

"My father and brother are both union supporters."

Rip smiled as if he knew something Jim didn't about Charlie and the editor.

"You like working here this summer, Jack?"

"Not especially," Jim said, and he went back inside the factory.

INFORMATION MEETING TONIGHT, 7:00. KING-DOM COMMON TOWN HALL. TO SEE WHETHER EMPLOYEES OF THE AMERICAN HERITAGE FURNI-TURE FACTORY WILL VOTE TO JOIN THE UNITED WOODWORKERS OF AMERICA.

"They're p-pretty as c-c-circus posters," Little Ti Thibideau said, nodding at the stack of three-colored posters the editor had just printed up.

"It will be a circus, all right," the Scout said. He looked at the poster he was holding as if it were a last will and testament disinheriting him of a long-expected legacy. "What's the damage here, editor?"

Jim's dad shook his head. "No charge. They're my contribution to the cause. Just be careful where you put them. Don't go on any private property without permission."

The editor let Jim borrow his DeSoto for the afternoon. Jim drove; the Scout rode shotgun; Ti, whom Jim had recruited to help distribute the notices, sat in back. They started out in the village, tacking the handbills onto the trunks of the elms around the perimeter of the green.

Next Jim drove out the county road along the Upper Kingdom River. Ti put up a few posters above the Public Fishing Waters signs on the bankside black willows. They hit Pond in the Sky, the Landing, and Memphremagog, up on the Quebec border at the foot of the big lake of the same name.

"Can I ask you something?" Jim said to the Scout. "How come you don't own a car?"

"I did, oncet," the Scout said. "One of Mr. H Ford's flivvers, spanking new off the line. Trouble is, owning a motorcar gives the enemy a hostage. First they egged her. Then they slashed the tires. Busted out the windscreen and cut the brake line. Finally they blowed her up with me at the wheel. Did you ever spend a month in the charity ward of the Wheeling Hospital, Jim? I don't recommend it.

"Oh, yes," the Scout went on. "I have been exploded in Wheeling, shot out of Matewan, and ridden on a rail through the hilly streets of Butte, Montana, in the distinguished company of Big Bill Haywood. I was stabbed in the gizzard with a meat hook in a packing plant in Lawrence. Pelted with overripe heads of cauliflower in Bakersfield. And pummeled half to death by the burly sergeant of arms of the John Birch Society in Tulsa, Oklahoma."

"J-J-Jesum Crow, mister," Ti said. "You m-must really b-b-believe in unions."

"What are them stone cribs out there in the river for?" the Scout asked.

"They're to keep the spring log drives from jamming up," Jim told him. "In the spring they float logs down out of the woods to the American Furniture mill."

"Company own the woods, does it?"

Jim nodded.

"Tell me the story, forest to showroom, of the making of an article of furniture, Jim. Say one of those trestle eating tables they want an arm and a leg for."

Jim did. But when he looked over at the Scout a few minutes later, A. J. Peabody's eyes were shut and his chin was resting on his collar. Jim doubted he'd heard a word.

The Scout didn't offer to pay Jim or Ti, or to reimburse the editor for gas, but at the end of the afternoon he went up to his room at the hotel and returned with a UWA cap for Ti.

Ti was overwhelmed. All he could say was, "Oh, you g-guys."

The Scout held up his hands and ducked his head to the

side as if dodging any gratitude that might come his way. "See you boys tonight at the hall," he said. "Seven sharp."

The information meeting to vote on whether to vote to join the union didn't start until close to 7:30. Men kept drifting in late, many with their hats pulled low. Some stood in the shadows in the back of the hall. Jim, Charlie, and Little Ti sat in the second row. At 7:25, the editor, who'd been elected by a voice vote to moderate the meeting, introduced A. J. Peabody.

The Scout came onto the stage like a man expecting a snake to slither out from under his feet at any moment. He pulled some notes from his jacket pocket, then put them away again. Something splattered on the stage near his polished shoes. An egg.

"None of that, now," the editor said. "We'll have civility or I'll adjourn this meeting."

The Scout stood still. Only when the hall was perfectly silent did he begin to speak.

"Name A. J. Peabody," he said. "Most call me the Scout. Born in Birmingham. Shifted to Gary with my people when I was three. Shifted to Flint. Shifted to Chicago. Came up rough on the streets of Chi-town. Landed in De-troit. Landed in Toledo. Currently employed by the United Woodworkers of America out of Peoria."

At the mention of the United Woodworkers of America, some of the factory workers clapped. Some, led by Rip Kinneson, booed. Again the Scout waited for quiet. When he resumed speaking, his voice was louder.

"Men, I'm going to tell you a story," he said. "Here it is. A man goes out in the winter woods of Vermont. He wades around in the deep snow until he finds a tall, straight pine tree. But this man doesn't see a pine tree. What he sees is a beautiful trestle-style eating table.

"Now, that's a very valuable tree, a tree that looks like a costly eating table. So the man looks around for a clear space to fell it and then he notches the tree and drops her on down. And it ain't one safe thing about that man's job of work because quick as nobody's business that great giant pine tree could swop around on its butt and take his head clean off. Or fall partway and get hung up on another tree, that's called a widow maker, then drop the rest of the way and crush that man to pulp. Oh, it's any number of ways that pine tree can kill that woodsman dead as Judas, including a hundred and one ways that he and I and you could never dream of until they happened. But they don't. Happen. Instead, that big old tree drops into that clearing neat as pie. Why for? Because *that worker knows what he is doing.* That's why for."

The Scout's voice had acquired a confident resonance. Everyone in the hall was listening intently as he continued to narrate how the woodsman limbed out the giant white pine and cut it into logs to be skidded to the riverbank and, come ice-out, driven down the river to the mill in the Common. He told the story that Jim had told him that afternoon, of the creation of the pine table, but when A. J. Peabody told it he made Jim shiver in the snow-filled woods and out on the icy whitewater of the Upper Kingdom, where red-shirted rivermen risked their lives on the drive. He made Jim hear the shrieking saws and planers and jointers in the mill. Jim could smell the good, clean scents of wood resin and glue and varnish, and the Scout made him see the trestle table and twelve ladder-back chairs created from a single pine tree by men who all knew what they were doing.

A. J. Peabody paused. Then in a quieter voice he said, "Who are those men?

"The loggers, the river drivers, the woodworkers? Why, they're you, boys. That's who."

And in a still quieter voice he said, "I want to ask you a question. How many of you own one of those top-of-the-line trestle eating tables? Throw up your hand."

Not a hand went up. The Scout nodded and said in a voice that was scarcely louder than a whisper, so that the crowd had to lean forward and strain to hear, "Jesus was a worker in wood."

"Yes!" Little Ti shouted like a mourner at a tent meeting.

"Yes is right," the Scout said, a little louder. Then, louder still, "Jesus of Nazareth was a woodworker. And if it had been a branch of the Woodworkers of America in old Galilee, why, they'd have saved him from his torments on the cross. The shop steward would have gone up to Pilate and said, 'See here, Mr. Pilate. You hammer that young street preacher up on that cross, by God, every union from Jerusalem to Bethlehem will sashay out on strike for a month of Sundays. I mean the stone-masons' union. I mean the shipbuilders' union. I'm talking about the vintners' union. We'll shut down your cities, your harbors, your vineyards. What'll you render unto Caesar then? Your head, that's what. You let that boy go free or else.' "

"That sounds to me like commonism," Rip Kinneson sang out.

"To me it seems like c-c-common sense," Little Ti Thibideau hollered.

"If the resurrected Lord Jesus Christ Almighty himself came to town tonight, there would be no seat for him at an American white-pine eating table," the Scout said. "That's all."

Next, several workers spoke from the floor. About half of them were in favor of a union. Rip Kinneson rose and suggested that General Douglas MacArthur be called in to clean house with the commie organizers.

"Put the flamethrower to them, Rip!" someone shouted. "You and General Mac."

Mr. Arthur Anderson spoke last. He said that the American Furniture factory had been the heart and soul of the village economy for more than a century. He said that the pieceworkers on the machine floor and in the cabinet room brought home hefty pay envelopes. Every employee received a turkey for Thanksgiving and a ham at New Year's. He reminded the members of the Outlaws that the factory bought their baseball uniforms and equipment.

Finally the frail old factory owner said that for several years he'd been borrowing money from himself to meet the weekly payroll at the factory. After all, God's Kingdom was his home, too. He'd been born and raised here. He didn't threaten to unbolt the machinery and ship it to South Carolina. He didn't need to.

As the union's local legal representative, Charlie handed

out paper ballots for the vote on whether to vote officially for or against the union. The editor, the Scout, Charlie, and Mr. Anderson counted the ballots: 164–137 to vote. Afterward the Scout, speaking privately to Charlie and Jim, called the outcome unpromising. He predicted that half of the yes voters would come down with a case of cold feet and cast no ballots on the straight up-or-down vote to be held thirty days later. In the meantime, he had a paper mill in Massachusetts and a textile mill in Rhode Island to visit. He left the following morning on the 5:08 combination and Jim didn't see him again for a month.

In the days to come, Little Ti Thibideau seemed to be here, there, and everywhere, talking up the union. He wore his UWA cap that the Scout had given him at work, at baseball practice, sitting out evenings with other workers on the beehive porch. On his way to the factory finish room each morning, he was careful to avoid passing through the mill floor, where Rip or one of his cronies might grab his beloved hat and throw it up a blower pipe. At lunch by the river he ate with one hand clasped on his cap, talking, talking, talking up the union, sometimes going on in French for minutes on end. Jim couldn't tell for sure, but when Little Ti spoke French he did not seem to stutter.

July passed quickly. The Outlaws were on a tear. Jim was on a tear, hitting over .500. He hadn't made an error at short all season. He no longer looked back over his shoulder after laying down a bunt or when he stole a base. He wished the

Scout would show up for one of his games, but there was no word at all from A. J. Peabody.

The week before the vote, Jim's father wrote a strong pro-union editorial in the *Monitor*. He cited the substantial profits of the American Furniture Company over the past five years. He pointed out that the company's two other plants, in Germantown, Pennsylvania, and Lansing, Michigan, were unionized. And reminded readers of the *Monitor* that the Anderson family owned more than twenty thousand acres of prime local woodlands. As for the old threat to move south, the editor posed a question. Where would the factory find workers, black or white, who had the skill and training to make the finest home and office furniture in the country? To train a single master machinist or cabinet-room woodworker required years.

Working pro bono, Charlie kept in close touch with the headquarters of the United Woodworkers of America in Illinois. He told Jim that the Scout would return to Kingdom Common as an observer at the polls. Charlie and the editor would be there as well.

"My father would have put your pal Peabody on the first train out of town," Mr. Anderson told Jim on his weekly inspection tour of the mill a few days before the vote.

Rip, standing nearby, said, "Your grandfather would have had him shot, Mr. A. Them was the days."

Mr. Anderson shook his head. "No, Herbert, I can't agree with you there. My grandfather and my father, too, to a degree, were ruthless men. Maybe they had to be. Times have changed since then, for the better."

"We need to take and make an example of somebody, Mr. A."

"We don't want to martyr anyone, Herbert."

"I weren't thinking of killing nobody. Just sending a message."

"Good day, Herbert. Good day, Jimmy. Keep up the good work. You'll get a story out of this job someday. I probably won't be around to read it, but I'd like to."

Just before ten o'clock break that morning Rip grabbed Jim by the elbow. "Jack," he said, steering Jim toward the stairs leading up to the finish room. "Go fetch Ti. I need him to match up some boards for me."

Matching boards to be ripsawed was one of Ti's specialties. Several times a week Rip called the fixer down to the mill floor to match together in grain and pattern the three or four boards that would be ripped for width, then glued together to form a special-order table or desktop into a single unit. Jim loved to watch Ti arranging different combinations of lumber in order to find exactly the right match. Sometimes the men at the planer and jointer would pause to watch as well. At first the match might not be obvious. Then it would dawn on Jim that Ti had found the perfect combination. How he did this no one could say, least of all Théophile Thibideau himself, any more than he could say how, with a chisel and a dollop of wood fiber, he could transform a damaged second into a top-of-the-line showroom piece.

Ti had a habit when concentrating on his work of sticking out the tip of his tongue. Rip Kinneson waited until Ti stuck out his tongue, then sidled up behind him, reached out quickly, and snatched off his UWA cap.

"No!" Jim shouted as Rip made as if to throw it up a blower.

"Okay, Jack," Rip said, and he tossed the cap toward the whirling ripsaw. Before Jim could stop him, Ti reached out to retrieve his cap and his unattached hand was flying through the air. It landed on the wheeled lumber truck with the table stock. There it sat oozing blood on the boards Ti had been matching.

Ti looked at his bleeding wrist. The shock was so sudden that he hadn't cried out. Bennett Carol was by his side, pulling off his own shirt to make a tourniquet. Bennett, Jim, and two other men from the mill floor laid Ti on a wide board and rushed him across the common to Doc Harrison's office. Doc said later that he might have been able to reattach a finger or thumb. Not a hand. He did stop the bleeding, and the make-shift tourniquet saved Ti's life, but his fixing days were over. As for the bloodstained boards on the lumber pallet, the only person who might have been able to reclaim them was fighting for his life in the county hospital.

"Go change the sign on the roof, Jack," Rip said when Jim returned to the mill.

" 'Zero Days Without an Accident.' "

It was the morning after the official vote. Jim and A. J. Peabody were waiting on the station platform for the 6:45 southbound. The Scout looked at his watch and said, "I detest a train that won't run on time. If there are two things in the world that I detest, it's a late-running train and a bold-faced lie."

Peabody jerked his head up at the sign on the factory roof, just coming into resolution in the dawn: "2 Days Without an Accident."

"That up there is a lie, Jim. It wasn't any accident. I and you both know it. It was a warning not to vote for the union."

"I guess it worked," Jim said.

"I reckon so," the Scout said. "Some places it might have backfired. Not up here."

The Scout frowned. "Like you say, Jim, fear is a powerful force."

"I didn't say that. You did." Jim said.

"Who said it doesn't matter," the Scout said. "It's true."

"Charlie said if he were county prosecutor, he'd have Rip Kinneson up in front of a judge faster than that saw took off Ti's hand."

"Hard to prove intent, Jim."

"I know what Rip's intent was. So do you. Listen, Mr. Peabody. What happened was my fault. I'm the one that asked Ti to help us put up those posters. And brought him down to the mill floor to match boards for Rip."

Jim thought the Scout might tell him not to be too hard on himself, but Peabody didn't. The southbound was pulling into the station. The door opened and the porter put down the step and reached for the Scout's carpetbag.

"Jim," Peabody said from the doorway, "I have been shot out of Matewan, rode out of Butte on a rail, and blowed up in

Wheeling, West Virginia. But this is the one place I've been that I can honestly say don't deserve a union."

The train was rolling again. In less than a week Jim would be back in school, and he was glad of it. He'd had enough experience in the real world for one summer. The 6:50 mill whistle blew, summoning the workers to their jobs. Jim headed across the tracks toward the factory to change the sign on the roof. Today was Day 3 without an accident.

10

Memorial Day

*Of all the splendid game fish of God's Kingdom, commend me
to the native brook trout. This tropically colored denizen of our
purest and coldest ponds, lakes, and rivers is abundant, hard-
fighting, and sublimely delicious. It was adopted by Charles
Kinneson I as the emblem for the family escutcheon, replacing
the Highland stag rampant, in 1768. Moreover, the copper fish
atop the weather vanes on both the Presbyterian and Roman
Catholic churches in Kingdom Common are unmistakably—
with their square tails, elegant proportions, and small, neat
heads—eastern brook trout.*

—PLINY'S *HISTORY*

Evenings in those years Jim loved to take his homework
over to Gramp's side of the house and spread it out on the
bird's-eye maple kitchen table Gramp had made Gram for a
wedding present. While Jim studied, at the other end of the
table Gramp would tie his brightly colored brook-trout flies—
flies with exotic names like Parmachene Belle, Queen of the
Waters, and Royal Coachman—or read in his Morris chair
beside the Home Comfort wood-burning range. Sometimes,

Jim would read one of his stories aloud to Gramp, as he'd read his very first stories about fishing and hunting and baseball to both of his grandparents before Gram died.

Gram passed away of pneumonia when Jim was eight. Gramp kept her ashes on the kitchen table in a large blue Dr. Bitters bottle that had once held a highly alcoholic patent medicine of that name. He referred to Gram's ashes as Our Lady of the Lake. "Just move Our Lady of the Lake onto the counter under her critters, Jim," Gramp said as Jim arranged his homework on the maple table. Gram's critters were the animals in the reproduction Gramp had given her many years ago of her favorite painting, Edward Hicks's *The Peaceable Kingdom.*

Because he'd loved Gram, Jim treasured her ashes in the Dr. Bitters bottle. He didn't find them macabre at all. When it came to the painting, he had mixed feelings. In it, several stylized animals—a lion, a tiger, a leopard, a bull, a wolf, and three sheep among them—stood or lay close together while a trio of otherworldly appearing children looked on. In the background, men resembling Pilgrims were conferring with several Indians. Printed neatly in the lower right corner of the painting was the verse from Isaiah that had inspired it. "The wolf shall lie down with the lamb, and a little child shall lead them."

Jim and Gram had been great pals. From birth she had been mute, and around her neck on a leather thong she wore a slate, like the desk slates children of her and Gramp's generation did sums and practiced making letters on. With a piece of chalk from her dress or apron pocket, she'd draw on the slate, in several deft, swift strokes, a tall stick lady and a little stick boy, holding hands. Above the lady and the little boy she printed the words "Gram" and "Jim." Then, below the figures, "Great pals."

Writing in chalk on the slate was how Gram communicated. She wrote each letter in reverse, working across the slate from her right to her left. Though she seemed to be writing backwards, the letters and words always appeared in the correct order.

Since Gram could not read to Jim, she selected books for him to read to her, as she had with Dad and Charlie. As a small boy, Jim had loved reading aloud to Gram. Robert Louis Stevenson. Mark Twain. Louisa May Alcott's *Little Men*. Jules Verne's *Mysterious Island*. And, of course, Jim's and Gram's favorite, Charles Dickens. Jim and Gram loved anything by Charles Dickens. There was no other writer like him and no story like *David Copperfield*, at least until Jim read *Great Expectations*. Dickens didn't *write* for his readers so much as *converse* with them. He wrote as though each of his readers was his very best friend, to whom he could freely tell absolutely anything. When Jim lay down to go to sleep, he could still hear, in his head, Dickens's magic sentences.

Jim was sure that Dickens would have had a field day with the Kinneson clan of God's Kingdom. He was just as glad that the great novelist hadn't gotten to some of his early ancestors first. His constant concern, as a boy, was that some other writer, looking for good stories to tell, would come sashaying up to the Kingdom and beat him to the punch. *Pliny's Ecclesiastical, Natural, Social, and Political History of Kingdom County*

alone would be a treasure trove of material. Gramp told Jim
not to worry. Even if a writer from away wrote the stories of
the Kingdom, they'd be written from "the outside looking
in." Jim, a Kingdom County Kinneson himself, already wrote
from the inside looking out.

When it came to books, Gram had what she called a guilty
pleasure: she loved to read murder mysteries. She'd read all of
Agatha Christie's many times over, and adored Daphne du
Maurier and Mary Roberts Rinehart. Also, the hard-boiled
detective stories of Dashiell Hammett, Raymond Chandler,
Ross MacDonald, and Mickey Spillane.

From the time Jim started school, Gram took him on the
train to the Saturday matinees at the old Paramount Theater
in Memphremagog, particularly when a new mystery was
playing. He cherished those afternoons with his grandmother
at the Paramount, with its shabby elegance, the worn plush
seats, faded velvet stage curtains, and roped-off balcony. He
loved the cartoons, the previews of coming attractions, even
the newsreels with their strident announcers and portentous
images of mushroom test clouds, hordes of Red Chinese, plug-
ugly strikebreakers with billy clubs and revolvers. Willie Mays
making a catch that couldn't be made. Joe DiMaggio's
picture-perfect swing, and Jackie Robinson stealing second.
There was no television reception in the mountains of God's
Kingdom during Jim's high-school years. The sports clips on
the newsreels at the Paramount were the closest he'd come to
seeing a major-league game.

When the killer made his first appearance on the screen,
Gram would nudge Jim with her elbow. She always spotted

the culprit long before anyone else. There was one mystery, however, that Gram had been unable to unravel. That was "Mad Charlie" Kinneson's motive for shooting his bosom friend, the Reverend Dr. Pliny Templeton, in their advanced years. No one in the family believed that "the trouble," as the murder was referred to on those rare occasions when it was mentioned at all, could be entirely explained by a disagreement over a piano. Mossbacked old dogmatist that he was, it was inconceivable that Charles would murder his adoptive brother over an obscure point of church doctrine. Why, then? Even Gram, the "Mrs. Arthur Conan Doyle of Kingdom County," as Dad sometimes called her, was stymied.

Like Jim's great-great-great-grandmother Molly Molasses, Charles I's wife, Gram had Indian ancestry. Plenty of Indian ancestry, to judge from her appearance, and from Dad's and Charlie's, as well. She had long, dark, straight hair; a dark complexion; and wide-set oval eyes as opaque as the big lake on the darkest night of the year. Dad and Charlie probably got their height from Gram, too. As Gramp liked to say, at just an inch under six feet, she stood as tall and straight as a princess.

Gram had some Indian ways, as well. She knew all of the names and uses of the wildwood plants of the Kingdom, from ginseng to pennyroyal. She could catch trout with her hands by reaching up under cut banks or submerged boulders, tickling their bellies, then sliding her fingers into their gills and yanking the fish out of the river. By putting her hands out of sight behind her back and taking one slow step at a time, she could walk right up to a curious young buck deer.

Gram had been an orphan. Gramp's parents, Charles II and

Eliza Kittredge Kinneson, had adopted her after the St. Francis
Orphanage across the border in Quebec had burned in the
Great Forest Fire of '82. Of all of Gramp's stories, Jim's
favorite was how, after the fire, Gramp and his father had
discovered Gram on the Île d'Illusion. Gramp, just five, had
ridden up the lake with his father in the bateau, looking for
survivors, hoping against hope that somehow Gramp's grown
sister, Mary Queen of Scots, had escaped from the fire, when
out of the lingering yellowish smoke, standing on the shore of
the island beside an unpainted skiff, they'd spotted a child,
a little girl surrounded by a dozen or so Jersey cows. No, not
cows. Deer. Deer watching Gramp and his father through the
smoke. A little apart, a half-grown black bear stood up on its
hind legs, like a circus bear, to get a better look at them. There
was a family of foxes, a bobcat, and two wolves, all of which
had evidently swum over to the island to retreat from the
flames. Around the child's neck on a thong was a slate on
which someone had written, *"Je m'appelle Jeannette St. Francis. Je ne parle pas."* The animals showed no signs of hostility.
Except for the soot on her face and hair and hands, Jeannette
seemed unharmed by the fire. There were no oars in the skiff.

Charles II picked up the child and returned to the bateau
and set her down on the bow seat next to Gramp. The two
children looked at each other for a moment as Gramp's father
tied the skiff by its painter to the iron ring bolted into the
stern of the bateau. Then he began to row back down the
lake through the smoke. Gramp reached out and took Jeannette St. Francis by the hand. The children were still holding hands when Gramp's father put into shore across the water

meadow from the Kinneson farmhouse. "Home, Jeannette," he said.

"From that day forward, we were inseparable," Gramp liked to tell Jim. Then he'd glance at the blue Dr. Bitters bottle and smile, more to himself, Jim thought, than to him, and say, "We still are."

It was the spring of Jim's junior year at the Academy, and Gramp had been feeling poorly all winter. Doc Harrison wasn't able to put his finger on just why. Old age, Gramp told Jim. Plain and fancy old age. No more, no less.

"Watch out for April," Gramp liked to say. April was the month when, having come through another Kingdom winter, elderly Commoners sometimes got caught leaning the wrong way like napping base runners. Sometimes they leaned so far in the wrong direction that they toppled right over into their graves.

April in God's Kingdom seemed to be an unlucky month in other ways, as well. April was when Jim's Abenaki ancestors had been massacred by Charles I and his Rangers. It was April when Charles's son, James Kinneson, and twenty of his fellow secessionists fought to the last man against more than three hundred federal troops dispatched to the Kingdom to put down their insurrection. And in the drought-stricken April of 1882 the village of New Canaan, established by fugitive slaves brought north by Gramp's father and Pliny Templeton, had been burned to the ground by the Ku Klux Klan.

To Jim's huge relief, Gramp survived April. But he didn't fish the rainbow run on the river with Jim and Prof, and he missed several of Jim's home baseball games. As May approached, it seemed doubtful that Gramp would be up to making their annual Memorial Weekend fishing trip to the wilderness ponds on the border.

"Limber up your fly rod, son," Gramp said one evening when the peeper frogs along the river were singing their hearts out. "I won't be running any footraces soon. But come Decoration Day, you and I'll be hitting out together. That record-book brook trout is still up there waiting for you to catch it."

For as long as Jim could remember, Gramp had promised him that if he caught a brook trout twenty inches long or longer, Gramp would have it mounted for him. Jim wasn't sure that there were any twenty-inch brook trout left in God's Kingdom to catch. But a trophy fish would be a bonus. What mattered was that he and Gramp would be going fishing together again.

Gramp had liked to say that the day for their trip picked them more than they picked it. On the Friday before the long holiday weekend it rained steadily all morning and on into the afternoon. That evening the wind backed into the northwest and the sky cleared. Gramp would have predicted a Canadian high, three or four days of sunny weather with falling water in the ponds and river. Falling water in the soft of the year, as Gramp called the days in late May when the hillsides and mountains of God's Kingdom were pale gold with newly opened hardwood leaves, was the best time to go brook-trout fishing.

Soon after sunrise on Memorial Day, Jim and Dad roped Gramp's Old Town to the roof of the family DeSoto and drove up the River Road to Pond Number One.

They carried the canoe to the water's edge. Jim got into the stern seat. Dad set the long-handled boat net, Gramp's pack basket, and a garden spade on the floor of the canoe. Then he gave the stern a push away from shore and Jim dug in his paddle.

There was a hatch of mayflies on the water this morning and the trout were rising to them. The brook trout in Pond Number One weren't large, but they were numerous and colorful, with crimson fins edged as white as Mom's Christmas paperwhites.

The first fish Jim hooked came straight toward the canoe, then jumped a foot out of the water. Before Jim knew what he was going to do, he'd reached out with the boat net and snared the leaping trout in midair. He knew he wouldn't be able to do it again in a hundred tries.

This time of year the Kinneson men, Gramp and Dad and Charlie and Jim, relied mainly on number-twelve, red-and-white Coachman flies that Gramp tied by the dozen over the winter at his kitchen table. Jim fished his flies wet, two or three inches below the surface, just as his Kinneson ancestors had done all the way back to the Hebrides. He believed that Gramp privately considered fishing with floating flies an elitist pursuit. Also, Gramp frowned on the catch-and-release practices of many of the anglers who came to fish in the Kingdom from away. In Gramp's opinion, trout were meant to be eaten, not caught and put back in the water to be caught again. Yet Gramp had taught Jim always to break the necks of his fish before dropping them into his creel so that they didn't suffer needlessly.

As Jim approached the collapsing log-driving dam at the outlet of Pond Number One, where he and Gramp had first seen the ridge runner, he reeled in his line and leaned his fly rod against the middle thwart of the Old Town. Jim studied the dam. "Hold on," he said aloud, and with several hard thrusts of his paddle, he shot the canoe through the gap in the dam where the sluice gate had been.

Jim caught more trout in the flow between One and Two, then fished his way up along the west side of Two. Today was turning into what Gramp would have called, in the camp journal, a good day on the water. Usually, fly fishing the river and ponds made Jim feel close to his grandfather and to the remote trout waters they both loved. Through his rod and line and the hard-fighting trout, Jim felt connected to the Kingdom itself. This morning he felt as moorless as an empty canoe on a windswept lake. It was hard to imagine that he would ever feel differently.

By the time Jim reached Three the trout had quit rising. The mayfly hatch was over and the sun glared on the water. Toward evening the fish would begin to feed again. "Let's see how the camp wintered over," Jim said. "Then we'll have a shore lunch."

The hunting camp with the words "God's Kingdom" carved into the lintel sat where Jim and Gramp had left it last winter.

Here on the northeastern slope of Kingdom Mountain the hardwoods were just coming out. Tiny red maple flowerlets littered the path from the shore up to the camp.

Inside, the air smelled of dead stove ashes. Jim swept some dried mouse droppings out the door. Then he penciled into the camp ledger:

Memorial Day, 1955. Opened camp after a good morning on the water. Jim Kinneson.

Gramp had an all-purpose saying: "You'll know what you're looking for when you see it."

The shelf on the wall behind Gramp's old-man's chair was wide enough. But it wasn't exactly what Jim was looking for.

He closed up the camp. Then he collected a handful of birch bark and hemlock stobs and kindled a driftwood fire on the gravel apron beside the pond in front of the camp. There he cleaned his catch. From the time Gramp had given Jim his first fishing knife, he'd loved to slit open the bladderlike stomachs of their trout and show Gramp what the fish had been feeding on. Today they were crammed with mayflies. A few hellgrammites and minnows. One lone peeper frog no larger than a dime.

Jim looked up the mountainside above the camp, where he and Gramp had gone to hunt deer and partridge and pick wild raspberries and blackberries in season. Partway up the mountain a stand of mature beech trees grew in a long-abandoned log landing. Gramp had taken him there many times to see the claw marks on the smooth gray bark of the trees where black bears had climbed up after beechnuts. In a damp depression nearby, a patch of pink lady slippers came up year after year. The year before Gram died Jim brought her here when the lady slippers were in blossom and offered to transplant a few to her flower garden. Gram had smiled. Then she'd written on her slate, "Let them stay home." The beech grove was a possibility.

Out of the pack basket Jim removed a number-fourteen black-iron spider, a loaf of Mom's oatmeal bread wrapped in waxed paper, salt and pepper, a pound of butter swaddled in cheesecloth, flatware, a crock of Mom's just-in-case baked beans—just in case the fishing was slow—a plain white crockery plate and a matching cup with a chipped handle, a tin of loose black tea, and an empty lard pail with a homemade wire bail for boiling water.

The pack basket was nearly two centuries old. Jim's Abenaki great-great-great grandmother had made it with a crooked knife from the inner bark of a white ash tree. When Jim was a little boy, Gramp had carried him on his back, standing in the pack basket, up the step-across brook above the camp. Gramp would hook a trout and pass his fly rod over his shoulder to Jim. Using both hands, Jim would derrick the thrashing little fish out of the water onto the ferns beside the bank.

Today Jim sat on a drift log on the scree beside the pond under a blue Canadian sky in the soft of the year and ate pink-fleshed trout with thick slices of homemade bread and butter washed down with black woodsmen's tea. He looked at the beautiful ash pack basket and wondered if he would have children and grandchildren to carry fishing in it. The pack basket was a link to the past. The future was as opaque as the surface of the ponds on the darkest night of the year.

Below Pond Number Three, the character of the river changed twice before it emptied into the big lake at the Great Earthen Dam. The first mile was fast and riffly, with natural stone-bars perpendicular to the current. In the fall of the year, when the brook trout ran both up and down the Lower Kingdom to spawn on the sand-and-gravel bottoms of the pools below the stone-bars, the fishing in this stretch of the river was superb.

Below the spawning pools, as the river entered the notch between Kingdom and Canada Mountains, it narrowed, deepened, and slowed to a crawl. Finally the current seemed to stop altogether. This was the Dead Water impoundment where Jim and Gramp had seen the river otter take the trout this past winter.

The Dead Water was the single stretch of the entire river that Jim didn't love. Here the Klan had surprised the former slaves of New Canaan at Sunday evening services with their families. Between ninety and one hundred New Canaanites were incinerated alive. A few others jumped out the windows. All but three were hunted down and slaughtered in the nearby forest.

The Great Earthen Dam had been built in 1900, creating the Dead Water and flooding out the charred remains of New Canaan. Jim felt that on the Dead Water in the notch between the mountains, he was in the presence of a great, lingering evil. But today he was determined not to dwell on the past or, for that matter, on the future. Today Jim had business in the present.

By the time Jim glided into the Dead Water, the afternoon sunlight was falling directly on the cliffs of Canada Mountain. Thirty feet to Jim's right, where the mountain plunged into its own upside-down reflection in the river, a thin curtain of water seeped down the face of the escarpment. Sometimes large trout lay in wait where the spring-fed rill washed aquatic life into the river.

Jim shipped his paddle and began false casting. He dropped his Coachman just above the junction of the waterfall and the river. What appeared to be a good fish, either a salmon or a very large trout, swirled at the fly but didn't strike. The Old Town or Jim's profile or the shadow of his leader on the water had spooked it.

Jim rested the fish. Then he picked up his Orvis again. Using his wrist as a fulcrum, the way Gramp had taught him, he began to false cast. When he straightened his arm, the loops of slack line in his lap hissed out through the metal guides of his fly rod. The Coachman ticked off the base of the cliff and the trout struck.

The tip of the Orvis bent to the water as the hooked fish made its first surge downriver. Jim raised the rod above his head, applying as much pressure as he dared. Gramp had liked to say that a bamboo Orvis had backbone. It would bend almost double. Handled properly, it would never snap.

A salmon or a rainbow trout would have jumped by now. Almost certainly this was a big native brook trout. Suddenly it turned and came fast back upriver. Jim reeled as quickly as he could to keep slack out of the line. He maintained the tension on his leader just this side of the breaking point.

The trout made two more runs. Then it was finished. Jim held the landing net a foot below the surface close to the side of the canoe in order not to scare the fish into a last desperate flurry. He eased the played-out trout over the net and lifted it shimmering onto the floor of the Old Town beside the pack basket. It was a hook-jawed male at least twenty inches long. A true record-book brook trout.

Jim thought of the mounted fish in the hotel barroom. Over the decades, their fins and tails had frayed and split. Their colors had faded. It was hard to tell the brook trout from the browns and rainbows.

The trophy fish was hooked lightly and there was no sign of blood. Jim reached into the net and removed the Coachman from the cartilage in the corner of the trout's mouth. He lifted the net with the trout in it over the side of the Old Town and turned the fish back out into the Dead Water. Briefly, it hung motionless, fanning its gills. Then it flicked its square tail and was gone, and at exactly that moment, Jim knew what he'd spent the day looking for.

Gramp had told Jim that their Abenaki ancestors were afraid of the big lake. The steep mountains on each side created a thirty-mile-long wind tunnel, so that on the calmest of days, when Memphremagog lay between the peaks as innocent as a mill pond, it could transform itself in scant minutes into a maelstrom. More than once, Jim and Gramp had seen it happen. For this reason, the Indians who came to the lake to fish in spawning season canoed it only in the early morning and near dusk, when the wind usually fell. Even then, they tended to stay close to shore, tracing its contours and rarely crossing open water.

This early evening in late May, dyed crimson by the reflection of the sunset, the lake was as unruffled as stained glass. A cathedral stillness enveloped its waters. A film of mist, pink in the sunset, hung over the Île d'Illusion as Jim approached it in the Old Town, and the island seemed to hover above the water in the mist, much as it had hung in the smoke from the forest fire three quarters of a century ago when Gramp and his father approached the crescent of beach where a silent child stood surrounded by wild animals.

The bow of the Old Town scraped on the pebbles. Jim stepped into the ankle-deep water and pulled the canoe out of the water. From the bottom of the pack basket in the bow he removed a rectangular cardboard box somewhat larger than a shoebox. "Jim, you'll know what to do with these," Gramp had written on the cover. Jim carried it and the short-handled garden spade up the slope through the woods to a small clearing overlooking the beach below. The floor of the woods was carpeted with caribou moss. Red-capped British soldiers grew on a decaying fallen tree. Elsewhere on the island, a few *habitant* French-Indian farmers grew potatoes and carrots in the sandy soil, and kept a small dairy herd and a maple orchard. Here at its southeast corner, the Île d'Illusion was still heavily wooded.

Twice he hit roots snaking out from the surrounding spruce and cedar trees. He'd have needed an ax to slice through them. On his third attempt, he got down three feet through the duff and hard soil. That was deep enough.

From the rectangular box, lined with crumpled back issues of the *Monitor,* he removed the blue Dr. Bitters bottle, heavier now than it had been when he'd transferred Our Lady of the Lake from Gramp's kitchen table to the counter below Gram's critters. He cradled the bottle in the bottom of the hole in the forest floor and sifted a cushiony layer of moss onto it and filled it in. He thought about saying something but didn't. From Gramp, Jim had learned everything he knew about storytelling. From Gram he had learned the eloquence of silence.

The sun had dropped behind the Canadian peaks to the west. The lake was a deep blue in the gathering dusk. Jim looked over the top of the Great Earthen Dam and up through the gap between Kingdom and Canada Mountains. He thought of the burned-out shells of the houses and the church, deep under the Dead Water impoundment. He thought of the hooded Klansmen galloping up the Canada Post Road. And he thought of the little girl who would become his grandmother, standing in the smoke with her kingdom of peaceable critters.

As he paddled back across the narrow strait between the Île d'Illusion and the mainland, Jim was more aware than ever that he dwelt in no peaceable kingdom. Yet out of the atrocities, out of the murders and hatred that made not a particle of sense, had come the almost accidental meeting of Gramp and

Gram, his Lady of the Lake, and their love for each other and for their family.

In the twilight the dam was an indistinct hulk, but Jim could make out Dad's DeSoto sitting on the gravel road beside the spur track. Dad was leaning against the front fender and smoking his pipe. He lifted his hand as the Old Town glided toward the shore and Jim lifted his hand in acknowledgement after a hard, good day on the water.

11

Senior Year

The Île d'Illusion is located in Lake Memphremagog about half a mile off the mouth of the Upper Kingdom River. Approximately five miles long by two miles wide, it was named by French explorers in reference to the uncanny way it seems to come and go in the lake mist, sometimes appearing to hover several hundred feet above the water, sometimes vanishing altogether.

—PLINY'S *HISTORY*

She was standing at the bottom of the granite steps leading up to the entrance of the Academy, wearing a dress of many colors, which appeared to have been made from a crazy quilt. The multicolored dress was cut short at her knees and she was tall and slender with shiny black waist-length hair. She had a dark complexion and wide-set eyes of so deep a shade of blue that at first Jim thought they were black. Over her shoulder she carried an old-fashioned bookstrap with a large volume buckled up in it. She was about Jim's age, seventeen, and so lovely that his heart hurt just to look at her.

On the top step, blocking the entrance, four sophomore

girls were skipping rope. Two of them were spinning the rope. The other two were jumping. All four were chanting an old local jingle:

Nigger girl, nigger girl,
Lives in Niggerville,
Way out yonder on Nigger Toe Brook.
Dat's de end of dis old book,
Dis old book 'bout Niggerville,
Way out back on Nigger Hill.

Prof Chadburn had forbidden the Academy students to use the word *nigger* but sometimes, out of his earshot, they did anyway. Now the girls were chanting the refrain:

Old black Pliny got two hole in him head.
Dat where Pliny got him ass shot dead.

The new girl narrowed her eyes, which had turned as purple as the big lake just before a storm. Nearby in the schoolyard a gaggle of kids looked on.

"Hey!" Jim yelled at the jump ropers. "Stop that."

He started up the steps to take the rope away from them.

"No!" the girl in the dress of many colors said. "I will deal with this matter. Hold my book, *s'il vous plaît.*"

She unbuckled the thick volume and handed it to Jim. He was surprised to see that it was Webster's dictionary.

"Niggerville, Niggerville," the jump ropers chanted.

The girl with the stormy eyes gave the bookstrap a hard

snap, cracking the metal buckle on the bottom step. She started
up the steps, twirling the strap buckle over her head. The
jumpers cut their eyes sideways at her as she advanced.

Whap. The buckle landed on the legs of one of the bullies.
Whap whap whap. The new girl struck blow after blow on
their arms and legs and shoulders as she drove them shrieking through the front door of the Academy.

"What wicked children, eh?" she said to Jim. "Very well. I
teach these *mals enfants* their first lesson of the day. Oh!
Excusez-moi! Je m'appelle Francine. Francine Lafleur."

Francine Lafleur placed one foot behind the other and
made a small curtsey, like a princess greeting a prince in one
of Jim's boyhood storybooks. Her eyes were deep azure again
and they were shining with delight as if she found the incident
with the rope skippers highly amusing. She held her arm out
straight to shake hands and her handshake was warm and
friendly.

"James Kinneson," Jim said. "Jim for short."

"You may, if you wish, address me as Frannie, James Kinneson," she said. "But I will never call you Jim for short. Now,
then. *À l'école, oui?* To school!"

While Jim walked Frannie upstairs to the senior homeroom, she told him that she lived on a farm with her parents
on the Île d'Illusion. Île d'Illusion was bisected by the international border between Canada and the United States. Children from the half-dozen farms on the island had their choice
of attending the French-speaking school in Magog, Quebec,
or the Academy in Kingdom Common. Few went beyond the
eighth grade, but Frannie had been fortunate. Her father's

older brother, Monsignor Lafleur, had invited her to board at the parish rectory in Magog and attend the Jesuit secondary school in that town. It had also been the Monsignor's idea for his niece to spend her senior year at the Common Academy in order to polish her English.

For as long as Jim could remember, senior homeroom had been held in the second-story science lab. This morning he and Frannie were the first students to arrive. The lab was furnished with Formica-topped tables and high stools instead of individual desks and chairs. It smelled of chemicals and musty animal mounts: a mangy Canada lynx, a great horned owl with fierce yellow eyes, a beaver gnawing on a poplar stick.

Suddenly Frannie grabbed Jim's arm. She was staring at the human skeleton dangling from a pole at the front of the room.

"That's just Pliny Templeton," Jim said. "The Negro guy in the jump-rope rhyme. He founded the Academy. In his will he left his skeleton to the school."

"My mother tells me her grandmother may have been a Negro," Frannie said. "She was born up the river in Canada, in the village that burned in the forest fire. *Ma mère* says that, except for my blue eyes, I look like this grandmother. Perhaps the evil girls jumping rope on the steps outside the school think so, too."

A little warily, Francine approached the bones. "How he receives these holes in his head, James Kinneson?"

Francine's eyes widened as Jim told her about the feud between his great-grandfather Mad Charlie Kinneson and the

Reverend Dr. Pliny Templeton, ending with Pliny's murder at the hands of his best friend.

Francine shook her head. "I do not believe this story."

"You don't believe Mad Charlie murdered Pliny? That's why he's known as Mad Charlie."

"Oh, I believe he murdered Pliny. But not over a piano, of all things. No, James. They quarreled over a woman. A very beautiful woman with whom they were both in love. I am certain of it."

"They were both old men at the time."

"Nevertheless. They fought over the love of a woman. But look, he is missing one hand. How is that?"

Frannie listened intently as Jim told her the story Miss Jane had told him, how Pliny had chopped off his own hand with an ax to free himself and search for his wife, who had been sold down the river.

"I knew it!" she said. "What did I tell you? Your Pliny was a man who gave everything for love. I intend to seat myself here, next to him. Perhaps I will become the new love of his life."

"I hope not," Jim said before he knew he was going to.

Francine smiled. Now her eyes were the lavender color of wood violets. She raised her dark eyebrows. "Well?"

"Well what?"

"Will you sit beside me?"

As Jim sat down, she opened her dictionary to the G section and began reading the first column of entries. From time to time her lips moved silently as she tried out an unfamiliar word.

Jim realized that Frannie was memorizing Webster's dictionary.

Each weekday in the dark before dawn, Francine rowed a homemade wooden boat across the water from the Île d'Illusion to the mainland. Near the Great Earthen Dam at the mouth of the Upper Kingdom River, she caught the morning milk train to Kingdom Common. She returned to the dam again on the late-afternoon northbound local.

Soon it became apparent that Francine was an outstanding student. Every day she mastered several pages of new words in her dictionary, which she carried with her everywhere. At a glance, she memorized entire scenes from *King Lear* and all of "The Rime of the Ancient Mariner" and Longfellow's "Evangeline." Using the entire blackboard, she outlined the principles of calculus to her senior math class.

A year ago, Charlie'd given Jim his old truck. As the leaves began to turn that fall, Jim started meeting Frannie at the dam and driving her to school. After school they took long rides along the hilly back roads of the Kingdom to view the fall colors. Jim asked her to the annual Harvest Ball at the Academy, which she attended in a blue gown she'd made herself, appliquéd with the northern constellations.

Jim canoed out to the island on weekends. Frannie Flower, as he'd begun to call her, was a born mimic, and captured perfectly Jim's abstract expression when he was writing in his head. Even her parents seemed a little in awe of her. They called her their *"fille mirabile,"* a miracle daughter born to them long after they'd given up all hope of having a child.

On a mild afternoon in mid-October Frannie took Jim to a glade on the knoll behind her house, overlooking a great sweep of the lake stretching far into Canada. In the clearing were nine lozenge-shaped cedar markers no more than a foot high and set close together, shoulder to shoulder, like meadow mushrooms sprung up after a summer rain. Carved into each of the wooden tablets was a name.

"Voilà!" Frannie said. "My older brothers and sisters, James. Arrived in the world months before their time."

Frannie walked from one marker to the next, bending over and touching each one. "This one, Philippe. Had Philippe lived, I believe he would have become a great teacher. His little sister, Michelle. She, a wonderful mother. *Regardez-vous, James. Ici est Jacques.* A gifted fisherman, I think, like the Christ."

She moved on down the row of markers, inventing a vocation for each of her stillborn siblings. "Listen to me, James. Being a *fille mirabile* is not always so easy. Born to an ancient mother and father, the only child of ten to survive? I must now live for ten. This I have decided to do by becoming a doctor. I will combat the terrible diseases of the world. The cancer. The stroke. The miscarriages like those of *ma mère*. Now you know my great secret. What is yours?"

Jim told her his plan to write the stories of the Kingdom. Frannie nodded. Then she took his hands in hers and looked into his eyes and for the first time they kissed, long and passionately, in the glade on the Île d'Illusion in the Lake of Beautiful and Treacherous Waters.

Jim loved sitting in the fall evenings beside Frannie at the plank table in her farmhouse kitchen, with its flagstone floor and great slate fireplace and smoky ceiling beams in which the adze strokes were still visible. Frannie had hand-painted local wildflowers around the tops of the white plaster walls, in the order of their blossoming: coltsfoot, spring beauties with lavender centers, paintbrush, daisies and brown-eyed Susans, chicory, cinquefoil, asters, and goldenrod. From the beams hung nets of onions and garlic bulbs from Madame Lafleur's kitchen garden and, by their roots, medicinal herbs that Madame and Frannie picked in the nearby woods. Between the two south-facing kitchen windows, one of Frannie's watercolors depicted the farmhouse with its Canadian-orange tile roof and the blue lake beyond, extending deep into Quebec between the mountains. Down the middle of the stone floor, from east to west, ran a straight black line representing the international border. During Prohibition, Réné Lafleur had operated a tavern out of the farmhouse. Customers could stand in the United States, on the south side of the black line, and order a whiskey or a beer. Then they could step across the line into Canada and legally drink it.

On holidays Frannie's uncle, the old Monsignor, visited. He and Réné sat at the kitchen table and drank quantities of Réné's hard cider and reminisced about their whiskey-running days, smuggling boatloads of Canadian booze down the lake from Magog. When American revenuers raided the

farmhouse, the young Lafleur brothers would sit on crates of
Seagram's and Molson's on the Quebec side of the line and
offer the G-men a free drink.

Sometimes, to amuse Jim, Frannie would engage her uncle, the prelate, in theological disputation. "If I could, *mon
oncle*, I would annihilate God's henchman, Paul. Paul was a
fraud, who changed his name from Saul, and invented a new
religion. 'Henchman,' James?"

Jim nodded. Frannie was up to the *H*'s in her dictionary.

"Also, I would like to wipe from the face of the earth that
crazed old John the Revelator."

"Mademoiselle!" Madame Lafleur said sharply.

Réné smiled behind his hand. The Monsignor winked at
Jim. "Saint Frannie of Memphremagog, our future physician,
is proof against her own arguments, Jim. For all of her heresies, if your friend my niece is made in God's image, God cannot possibly be as bad as she says, eh?"

"I guess it takes a great deal of faith to be a believer, Father," Jim said.

"I would prefer to have a great deal of penicillin," Frannie
said. "To treat the mortal infections with which God has
blessed us. Only consider, James. The good Christ had a great
deal of faith. He had faith that his all-powerful father, the Ca-
liph of Heaven, would protect him. Look where Christ's faith
got Him. Pinned up on a cross."

"What do you think Jesus would do if He came here to
God's Kingdom today?" the priest asked Frannie.

"Depart on the first train out," Frannie said. "Before God
could get His hands on Him."

The Monsignor, whose personal library at the rectory in Magog was well-stocked with Voltaire, Rabelais, and Balzac, and who was something of an iconoclast himself, roared with laughter. *"Bien!"* he said. "As our beloved Dame Julian of Norwich said, 'All shall be well, and all manner of things shall be well.' Of this, I am certain."

"If that is what Dame Julian truly thought, she was in for a very unpleasant surprise," Frannie said.

Réné looked at Frannie with a degree of awe. Madame pursed her lips and frowned, but Jim could tell that she, too, was enormously proud of her daughter the miracle child.

As for Jim's own parents, the editor and Ruth had fallen in love with Frannie the day Jim brought her home to meet them. Like Athena Allen, Frannie was the daughter they'd never had. At the same time, Mom surprised Jim, and embarrassed him somewhat, by giving him a package of condoms, "just in case."

"I guess you know teenage boys," Jim said.

"I do, sweetie," Mom said. "Teenage girls, too. After all, I was one."

The lake froze over in January. Frannie walked to and from the island over the ice. At school she continued to be deeply intrigued by the story of Pliny Templeton. Why were there no references in Pliny's great *History of Kingdom County* to his own history? To his youth in slavery before he fled north to freedom? How did one apply for the Templeton Scholarship awarded each year by the state university? One didn't,

Jim explained. It was presented at graduation to the top-ranking senior at the Academy. Frannie continued to insist that Jim's great-grandfather Mad Charlie Kinneson had murdered Pliny over the love of a woman. "Mark my words, James," she said. "It is the way of the world."

On weekends Frannie helped her father run his trapline along the Upper Kingdom River. Early in January, René Lafleur sprained his ankle in a beaver run. For the next two weeks Frannie stayed home from school to tend his traps. One Saturday, Jim accompanied her on her circuit. Trapping had been an important source of cash income for generations of Lafleurs. Even so, Jim was surprised by the matter-of-fact way Frannie, who loved all animals, hauled up the drowned muskrats and beavers in her father's sets. Near the shore of Pond Number Three, across the ice from the hunting camp, they came upon a snarling fisher, caught in a trap baited with chicken skin at the base of a giant hemlock. In its determination to free itself, the animal had nearly chewed off its own back leg. Dispassionately, Frannie put the fisher out of its misery with a fireplace poker she carried in her pack basket and referred to as "Our Merciful Savior." "And *merci* to you, too, Monsieur Fisher," she told the dead animal. "Your gorgeous pelt will pay for my books at university this fall."

Gramp would have understood, Jim thought. As a boy growing up on the farm that wasn't, Gramp had run his own trapline, using the proceeds to buy his books and school clothes.

Late that afternoon, a snow squall came roaring down out of Canada. Jim and Frannie took shelter in the camp. Jim built a fire in the Glenwood, and they made love in the loft where he'd spent so many nights as a boy on hunting and fishing excursions with Dad and Gramp and Charlie. Afterward, Frannie cried a little, Jim hoped from happiness. Then, propped up on her elbow, she said, "Now, James, we are lovers, like Pliny and the secret love of his life, whoever she may have been. Also, we are adversaries for the Templeton Scholarship. Fierce rivals by day, passionate lovers by night. How romantic! But you must know that if you let up in your studies and allow me to win the award, I shall have no choice but to hunt you down with Our Merciful Savior and dispatch you as I did the noble fisher. That would be disagreeable for me and more so yet for you."

"What about your physician's oath, Dr. Lafleur?"

"What about it? When I become Dr. Lafleur, I will do no harm."

"Frannie Flower, I never know when you're joking and when you're serious."

"I have never been more serious in my life. If you let me win the scholarship, out of the pack basket comes Our Merciful Savior. You may depend upon it."

"I won't let up, and you may depend upon that," Jim said, and he took her into his arms again.

That winter and spring Jim and Frannie made love at the farm that wasn't whenever his folks weren't home. Charlie gave Jim the key to his office on the fourth floor of the courthouse and they made love there, inventively and frequently. They went parking in Jim's pickup on back roads all over the county, especially to the pull-off on the height of land south of the Landing, beside the granite obelisk inscribed with the warning "Keep Away." Sometimes at night, from the top of the ridge, they could see the rose-tinted reflection of the lights of Montreal on thin clouds above the city, and the crimson and blue, silver and saffron flares of the northern lights far to the north over the Laurentian Mountains. "I think, James, we made that happen. The aurora."

Once, after school hours, they made love in the science room of the Academy. "Well, Monsieur Pliny," Frannie said afterward, "as you can plainly see, with us all is well. Is all well with you? Are all manner of things?"

"What did he say?" Jim asked her.

"He said not by a long shot, they aren't. He said he wasn't telling us what to do, but in our place he'd gather his rosebuds in the here and now."

In February, Jim and Frannie ice-fished on the big lake. In March they helped her father sugar off. Late in April an all-night rain swept in on the back of a south wind, and the ice went out of the lake in three booming explosions.

Their senior year was winding down. Like many boys, Jim excelled in subjects that interested him. English, Latin, and history, in his case. In his other classes he did what he needed to do to get by. He finished his high-school career with a cumulative average of 92.5, well behind Frannie's top-ranking 98. As class valedictorian, she would receive the Templeton Scholarship to attend the state university. Jim was offered a partial baseball scholarship and a part-time job in the university library. He'd never doubted that Frannie would win the Templeton Award and was delighted that they'd be attending college together.

But on the day before graduation, as Jim was helping his father run off programs for the ceremony, George Quinn, chairman of the Academy board of trustees, appeared at the *Monitor* with stunning news. Francine was ineligible for the Templeton Scholarship. The original agreement between the university and the Academy stipulated that the recipient must be an American citizen. "There's no birth certificate for the Lafleur girl on file at the county clerk's office or the Vermont Department of Health, editor," George said. "Unless she can produce one herself, it looks like Jimmy's next in line for the award."

"Goddamn it, George," the editor said. "Anyone born on Mirage Island is automatically a dual U.S.–Canadian citizen."

"Actually, Charles, the school never really had to accept her in the first place. I mean, being part Indian and part Negro, too, for all we know."

"George, are you familiar with the recent Supreme Court ruling *Brown* vs. *the School Board of Topeka, Kansas?* The local school district, that's the Academy in this instance, is legally obligated to accept and offer full privileges to all children residing in the district. Mirage Island is in the school district. Réné Lafleur pays U.S. taxes and Vermont taxes."

"That's so," George said. "But don't you see, Charles? Without an authentic birth certificate, we don't have any official record where the girl was born. Our hands are tied. It's a black-and-white matter."

"You're right about that, George," the editor said. "That's exactly what it is. Jim, go over to the courthouse and get your brother. I don't care if he's in the middle of the trial of the century. Go get him now."

The following morning, half the village turned out to hear Charlie's petition to the new judge, who was still referred to as "the new judge" after two years, to issue an injunction awarding the Templeton Scholarship to Frannie. The Academy trustees had legal representation, as well. They'd hired Zack Barrows, the recently retired prosecuting attorney of Kingdom County. Jim sat directly behind Charlie and Frannie at the plaintiff's table, with Frannie's parents and her uncle, the Monsignor. He'd asked his father to let him cover the special court hearing but the editor had said no. That would be a conflict of interest, or at least give the appearance of one. Dad would cover today's proceedings himself.

Charlie's first witness was Prof Chadburn. "Prof," Charlie said, "I'd like to begin by asking you to state your full title."

"I'm headmaster of the Kingdom Common Academy."

"How long have you held that position?"

"Too long. Forty-one, going on forty-two, years. Thankfully, I'm retiring at the end of this term."

"So for more than four decades, through wind and rain and sleet and snow, you put up with young rapscallions like me. I'm impressed."

"Well, Charlie, in all honesty, I'm afraid I'd have to say

that I never knew any other boys quite as troublesome as you. You were in a league of your own."

General laughter.

"Well, you know what they say, Prof. Some very bad boys grow up to be very good men."

"I can assure you from a fair amount of experience that most don't," the new judge interrupted. "Mr. Kinneson, make your point."

It was evident to Jim that the new judge did not care for Charlie or, for that matter, for his assignment to Kingdom County. Charlie himself had said he didn't blame him. Who'd want to adjudicate in a place whose motto for two centuries had been "Keep away"?

"Certainly, your honor," Charlie said. "Prof, could you please describe the Templeton Scholarship?"

"It's a full four-year scholarship, all expenses paid, to the state university in Burlington. It's awarded annually by the university to the Academy graduate with the highest cumulative four-year average. It's given in honor of Pliny Templeton, whom the university claims as the first American Negro college graduate."

"Who is the top-ranking student this year?"

"Francine Lafleur. She ranks first in her class by more than five percentage points."

"Thank you, Prof. Your honor, I'd like to call George Quinn."

After the president of the Academy trustees was sworn in, Charlie asked him if there were any additional eligibility requirements for the Templeton Scholarship.

"Just one," George said. "It stipulates that the recipient must be an American citizen. Miss Lafleur hasn't been able to prove to the trustees that she was born in the United States."

"How would she do that?"

"With an American birth certificate. Unfortunately, she hasn't been able to produce one."

Next, Charlie called Francine, who was wearing her blue dress with silver constellations embroidered on it. To Jim, she looked more beautiful than ever.

Frannie stated her name and address, Mirage Island.

Charlie said, "Miss Lafleur, is Mirage Island located in the United States or Canada?"

Frannie smiled. "Both."

"How can it be located in two countries at the same time?"

"Well, Charlie Kinneson, you must know that the international border between Vermont and Quebec, as established by the Webster-Ashburton Treaty, is the forty-fifth parallel of latitude. The forty-fifth parallel of latitude cuts directly through Mirage Island. South of the parallel is the United States. North is Canada."

"And your family's farm is located?"

"Directly on the parallel. The line is painted through the middle of our kitchen."

"Thank you, Miss Lafleur. That's all. Your honor, I'd like to call Miss Lafleur's mother, Mrs. Madeleine Lafleur, to the stand."

Madame Lafleur, in her black church dress, came forward and took the oath.

"Mrs. Lafleur, you heard your daughter testify that the

international border runs directly through your kitchen. It's represented by a painted black line."

"*Oui*. I pass from the United States to Canada and back again one dozen, two dozen times a day."

"Which side of that line was Francine born on?"

"The south. Our bedchamber is off the parlor on the north side. So for the birth of Francine, we move the bed into the kitchen, south of the line. In the United States."

"Were there any other witnesses, besides you and your husband, that Frannie was born south of the line?"

"*Oui*. The midwife. But when we come with the midwife to the county clerk here in this courthouse, to have made a certificate of birth for Francine, your clerk refuses to allow the midwife to speak because she is Canadian, not American. So we are never able to receive the certificate."

Zack Barrows got to his feet. "Your honor, I object to all this hearsay. Without an American witness, the girl and her parents can't prove where she was born. Therefore, she can't procure a birth certificate. Without a birth certificate proving that she's an American, she isn't eligible for the Templeton Scholarship."

"Mrs. Lafleur," the judge said. "You have no other witness who could testify where your daughter was born?"

"*Oui*. Is one other witness."

"Besides your husband?"

"*Oui*. Yes. Besides."

"And who would this other witness be?"

"God," Madame said. "The island, Île d'Illusion, this village, your county, it is all, as they say, God's Kingdom. God is our witness that Francine was born in His Kingdom."

"Well, I don't believe God is available to testify this morning," Zack said.

Beside Jim, Frannie's uncle, the old bootlegger-Monsignor, got to his feet. "Your honor," he called out. "As God is *my* witness, He is here this morning. God is everywhere. This we would all do well to remember."

The new judge and former marine major looked as if he wished he were back on Pork Chop Hill. He looked as if he wished he were anywhere other than God's Kingdom.

"Your honor," Charlie said hurriedly. "There's a precedent that goes back to a verbal but binding agreement between Daniel Webster and Lord Ashburton that anyone born on Mirage Island is de facto a dual U.S.–Canadian citizen. Neither the school trustees nor anyone else has produced any proof that Frannie Lafleur, the valedictorian of the Academy graduating class of 1956, is not an American citizen."

"Your honor," Zack said, "no one can prove a negative. We need proof of citizenship. Until the girl can show the trustees a birth certificate, their hands are tied."

"Well, I can understand that," the new judge said. "While I fully acknowledge that there is a great deal, a very great deal indeed, about Kingdom County, Vermont, that I do not, and probably never will, comprehend, I can and do understand why the trustees of the Kingdom Common Academy need to see an American birth certificate for Mr. Kinneson's client in order to award her the scholarship. And now I will share a little story with you. I can understand this in part because my own parents, Antonio and Rosa Paglia, came to this country from Sicily. I was born the next year and I will assure you that they immediately obtained an American birth certificate for me."

Jim's heart fell. When the judge had revealed that his parents had been immigrants, Jim had felt hopeful. But only momentarily. Antonio and Rosa Paglia had done everything according to the letter of the law. Clearly, Judge Paglia was going to rule against Francine.

"So, Mr. Barrows," the judge continued. "This is your lucky day. It is your lucky day and it is the lucky day of the Academy trustees. Because if all you need to see in order to award Miss Lafleur the scholarship is an American birth certificate, I am going to arrange for you to see one. Mr. Kinneson, I'd like for you to go down to the county clerk's office on the second floor and bring back the clerk, Mrs. Kittredge. Kindly tell her to bring a blank birth certificate and her official stamp along with her. I intend to order the county clerk, Mrs. Kittredge, to issue Miss Francine Lafleur a birth certificate stating her place of birth as Mirage Island, Kingdom County, the State of Vermont, the United States of America. Right now."

"Your honor," Zack said. "She isn't even *white*."

"Neither, as I understand it, was Pliny Templeton," Judge Paglia said. "Miss Lafleur," the judge continued, "I would like to be the first to congratulate you. You are the 1956 recipient of the Pliny Templeton Scholarship. If I may add a personal note, the state university will be most fortunate to have you as a student. You will do them, and us, proud."

"Your honor, I object. These proceedings are an outrage."

Bang! Down came Judge Paglia's gavel. "Mr. Barrows," he said, "on that point, we are in total agreement."

In accordance with a tradition dating back to the founding of the Academy as a Presbyterian institution, graduation was held at the now United Church at the south end of the village green. The following afternoon at precisely two o'clock, the twenty-eight members of the class of '56 filed into the church to the labored strains of "Pomp and Circumstance" on the ancient organ. Proudly, and a little self-consciously, the seniors seated themselves in the first two rows of pews. Directly behind them sat their teachers and the Academy trustees. Then family and friends. The soon-to-be graduates were aligned in alphabetical order. Frannie sat next to the center aisle in the first pew. Jim sat beside her.

It seemed to Jim much longer ago than just yesterday that Judge Paglia had ordered the town clerk to make out an American birth certificate for Frannie, and the school trustees to award the Templeton Scholarship to her.

Frannie, however, had news of her own. Earlier that year, on the advice of Prof Chadburn, she'd submitted a backup application to McGill University in Montreal. Recently, she'd learned that McGill had offered her a full scholarship to attend its premed program. For the time being, her citizenship status was a moot point. Jim, for his part, was relieved for Frannie, but devastated that they wouldn't be going to college together.

During the opening exercises Jim looked around at the white wainscot paneling and plain glass windows decreed by his stern Presbyterian ancestors. How many hundreds of tedious hours had he spent sitting on these hard wooden pews? Whoever invented church had done boys no favor. Moreover, the United Church of Kingdom Common had a particularly unsettling feature left over from its Presbyterian days. Suspended from the ceiling over the pulpit on a long metal rod was a most curious acoustical device known as a sounding board. The board was actually a hollow wooden box, about six feet in diameter and a foot deep, octagonal-shaped, with holes an inch apart drilled in its top, bottom, and sides. Its purpose was to amplify the minister's voice. The sounding board was affixed to the base of the rod by a carved wooden hand gripping a brass handle and known as the "Hand of God." Though very exact and lifelike, the hand had an otherworldly, genderless eeriness about it. The Hand of God, which was rumored to have carved itself, looked like a hand that would very gladly smite down an infidel city or two, much less an inattentive congregant. Anyone who doubted it needed only to read the legend carved into the outward-facing side panel of the sounding board:

The Board casts the Dominie's voice on high,
But should that Cleric tell a lie,
The Hand of God lets go.

The Board descends on the man below.
The Dominie dies.

Although Jim was no longer afraid of the Hand of God or of the sounding board, he detested them both, and viewed them as emblematic of everything that was harsh and rigid about the beliefs of his ancestors. Why the church trustees hadn't removed them decades ago he couldn't imagine.

The graduation ceremony began with a lengthy invocation in which Pastor John Wesley Kittredge, who disapproved of young people in general and teenagers in particular, gave the graduates and God alike some stern marching orders. Next came the presentation of a framed citation to Prof, who was retiring after forty years as headmaster of the Academy. A few modest local scholarships were awarded. Lizzy Kittredge won the Daughters of the American Revolution Scholarship. Jim had to smile. He knew from Pliny's *History of Kingdom County* that the first local Kittredges were Tories who'd fled Massachusetts in 1776. They'd settled in the Kingdom supposing that they'd reached Canada and sanctuary. No mention was made of the Templeton Award.

It was time for Frannie's valedictory. Prof introduced her by announcing that she was the best student he'd ever taught, and congratulating her on her scholarship to study at McGill. As she approached the pulpit, the entire class of 1956 rose and applauded. She did not seem to have a prepared text to speak from but was carrying her dictionary.

"Ladies and gentlemen, *mesdames et monsieurs*," Frannie began. "My fellow graduates, parents, families, and guests. I would like to introduce you to a dear friend. *Un moment, s'il vous plaît."*

Frannie walked across the dais and drew aside a plain dark curtain. Next to the sideboard where the communion service was stored stood what looked like a tall birdcage covered with a white sheet. Frannie carried the sheeted object back across the dais and set it down beside the pulpit.

"Voilà!" she said, and whipped off the sheet. Dangling from its pole was the skeleton of Pliny Templeton.

Frannie stepped behind the pulpit and opened her dictionary to a page near the back. "'Valedictory,'" she read. "'A farewell address.' The title of this year's farewell address is 'God's Kingdom.' I believe that the term was coined by our good friend here, the Reverend Dr. Templeton himself. So I pose to you a question. Who, exactly, was Pliny Templeton?"

Frannie paused, giving the people gathered in the church a moment to consider her question. "As we all know, Pliny was born into slavery. At about the age of thirty, with the help of Charles Kinneson II, the man who would become his closest friend and great *benefactor"*—Frannie smiled and tapped her dictionary—"he made his way north to freedom on the Underground Railway. Here in Vermont, again with the assistance of Charles, Pliny became the first Negro to graduate from an American college. Congratulations, Dr. T!"

Frannie removed her mortarboard and placed it on the skeleton's skull. From the pews, scattered chuckles and a smattering of applause.

"After receiving his Doctor of Divinity degree from the

seminary at Princeton, Dr. Templeton assumed this very pulpit, as minister of the Reformed Presbyterian Church of Kingdom Common. He founded, built, and was the first headmaster of the Kingdom Common Academy. He went to the Civil War as Chaplain of the Vermont 142nd Regiment. At the Battle of Gettysburg he seized a fallen officer's sword and helped beat back Pickett's charge."

From a shelf in the pulpit Frannie produced a military-style kepi from the Civil War era. She set the kepi on top of Pliny's mortarboard and snapped off a smart salute. This time the laughter and applause were general.

"After the war, Pliny introduced the sport of baseball to Kingdom Common. On the village green he laid out the first baseball diamond in New England. 'Baseball Pliny,' he was called."

Frannie reached into the pulpit again, like a magician reaching into a hat. This time she pulled out Jim's ball cap, which she balanced on top of the kepi and mortarboard on Pliny's skull.

"During Reconstruction, Dr. T returned to the South with some of his own students and established schools for freed slaves. He even found time to write a great book, *The Ecclesiastical, Natural, Social, and Political History of Kingdom County*."

Frannie turned to address the skeleton directly. "You did indeed wear many hats, Monsieur Templeton. Preacher, teacher, soldier, scholar. You were each of those and more. And yet, though you told in your *History* the entire story of the place you named 'God's Kingdom,' you recorded almost none of your own history. You never wrote the story we wanted most to hear: your own.

"Why did you never tell your story?" Frannie said. "Were you ashamed of your early life as a slave? It would not be surprising if you had been. Was that not one of the chief aims of that most wicked of all human institutions? To shame its victims?"

Frannie regarded the skeleton in the three hats. She shook her head. "I think, Dr. Templeton, that you were not ashamed. You were, after all, a proud man, and a brave man. Why, then, your silence about yourself? I believe that I know the answer. I believe that you felt that if you were to succeed with your great works here in God's Kingdom, you would need to pass for white. Correct me if I am mistaken."

Frannie held out her hands palms up, inviting the skeleton to correct her. She turned to the audience. "You see, *mes amis*. He remains silent.

"Of course, Dr. T, years after your death, when the university found it convenient to claim you as America's first Negro graduate in order to *aggrandize* their own reputation, they were quick enough to do so. They even established a scholarship in your name. Yet you, Pliny, felt unable to claim yourself. And in that assumption you were undoubtedly correct. A place settled as the result of the massacre of a band of unarmed Indians? A place that stood by and did nothing to prevent the annihilation of an entire community of fugitive slaves? A place that built a great towering dam in order to flood and conceal the evidence of where those former slaves were murdered? To be sure, Pliny, everyone in God's Kingdom knew very well that, like the residents of New Canaan, you, too, were a Negro. One glance at you would have told them as much. This we know from your handsome portrait in the lobby of the Academy. But as long as the matter of your race never came up, God's Kingdom was willing to look the other way because you were useful to them. And then, in your ancient years, after you had served out your usefulness, you were killed, for reasons we can only guess at, by the very man who helped raise you from slavery.

"*Mesdames et monsieurs.* It may be *presumptuous*"— Frannie gave her Webster's another pat—"it may be 'excessively forward' of me, a 'Black French' girl from the so-called Indian Island, with not only Abenaki but very possibly Negro blood running through my own veins, a girl greeted on the steps of Pliny's school last fall as a 'nigger from Niggerville,' to speak on behalf of Vermont. So be it. I will not do so. But while Frannie Lafleur may not be a Vermonter or even, in the opinion of some in this church, an American, her ancestry here in God's Kingdom goes back not just to the Revolution, and its daughters and sons, but thousands of years before that. So, Dr. Templeton, on behalf of God's Kingdom, I apologize to you. We apologize to you. God's Kingdom begs your forgiveness for forcing you to deny and ignore your own identity."

A faint breeze found its way into the church through the leaky window casements. *Click.* Pliny's feet tapped together like the most delicate of billiard shots. Otherwise, the church was as silent as the forests of God's Kingdom on a windless midnight in January.

Frannie pointed upward, at the sounding board suspended above her by the unearthly Hand of God. "If one word that I have spoken to you today is a lie, may the Hand of God release its grip this instant."

From the church pews came a collective gasp. In the ensuing stillness, Frannie waited for perhaps ten seconds. Then she said, "*Merci,* and farewell," and rejoined her classmates.

Pastor John Wesley Kittredge offered the age-old benediction. "May the Lord bless you and keep you and make His light to shine upon you." At a signal from Prof, the seniors rose and walked down the aisle and out of the church.

Graduation was over.

It was dusk in God's Kingdom. The lake lay still in the twilight. Half a mile off shore, the Île d'Illusion came and went in the mist. Somewhere nearby, a large fish broke the surface.

"Now then, James Kinneson," Frannie said. "My summer classes at McGill start not tomorrow but the day after. In the morning I depart on the train for Montreal. I intend to complete my undergraduate studies in three years. Perhaps in two. Then on to medical school. You, meanwhile, will attend the state university. Pliny's university. There you will continue to write the stories of God's Kingdom. If you do not"—she shook an imaginary poker in the air— "Our Merciful Savior!"

She threw her arms around Jim's neck and kissed him. Then she got into her boat and began rowing. She disappeared in the mist, appeared again briefly, vanished altogether. For a minute Jim could hear the creak of her oarlocks. Then nothing.

Jim stood alone on the lakeshore. He hoped that he and Frannie Lafleur might eventually find a way to be together, but he knew, at eighteen, that the future was as invisible as Mirage Island. For now, all he could do was drive back to the village and return Pliny's skeleton to the science room at the Academy, as he'd promised Frannie he would do. Like graduation, his senior year lay behind him.

12

God's Kingdom

God's Kingdom? I thought they called it that because only God would want the place.

—CHARLES KINNESON, EDITOR,
The Kingdom County Monitor

J im pulled out of the dooryard of the farm that wasn't in the pale light before the sun. It was Labor Day in God's Kingdom, and he was on his way over the mountains to the university.

The wild asters and goldenrod in the meadow along the river, where four years ago he'd encountered Gaëtan Dubois and his parents, were just acquiring color in the dawn. The river was invisible in its own fog, but the swamp maples along its banks were already showing sprays of red. Soon the brook trout would don their matrimonial attire, in preparation for their annual fall spawning ritual.

For Jim it had been a busy, lonely summer. To take his mind off Frannie, he'd thrown himself into his work at the *Monitor*.

In addition to the constant round of selectmen's and school board meetings, court arraignments, fairs and old-home days, car wrecks, and ball games on the common—"Outlaws Remain Undefeated with 10-1 Win over Pond in the Sky"—not to mention the appearance on the village green of a snapping turtle as big around as a washtub with "Charles Kinneson 1765" carved into its shell (Jim detected his brother Charlie's handiwork in the date and signature), there had been several unexpected developments to cover over the short northern summer.

In late June, the Common and its longtime enemy, Kingdom Landing, had voted to build a new consolidated high school midway between the rival villages. No one in God's Kingdom had ever imagined that such a thing could happen. Two weeks later, all passenger service on the Boston and Montreal Line running through the Common was terminated. Jim could see the time coming when rail freight service would end as well. There was talk of the Eisenhower interstate system reaching the Kingdom, and a ski resort on Jay Peak.

One morning in early August, Mr. Arthur Anderson keeled over at his desk at the factory. His sons, who ran the firm's sister plants in Michigan and Pennsylvania, shut down the mill on the day of their father's funeral. It never reopened. "Closed," the sign on the roof read.

Pliny Templeton had written in his great book that in the Kingdom, all history was Kinneson family history. Over the summer Jim had done a series of articles for the *Monitor* on

his ancestors. He'd written about the massacre of the Abenaki Indians by his great-great-great grandfather Charles Kinneson I, and the defeat and death of Charles I's son, the
secessionist James, at the second-longest covered bridge in the
world in 1836. Another article chronicled Charles II's rerouting of the outlet of Lake Kingdom. Yet another described the
burning of New Canaan and three million acres of border
country by the Ku Klux Klan.

Jim's favorite piece was the three-part biography he'd written of Pliny Templeton himself. A condensed version had
been syndicated by the Associated Press. Jim hoped someday to write a novel about Pliny.

He crossed the red iron bridge and came into the Common on the county road. As he headed south between the east
side of the village green and the Academy, he noticed a light
in the headmaster's office. On impulse, he pulled into one of
the diagonal parking slots in front of the playground. As Jim
walked up the granite steps of the school, it seemed just yesterday that he'd first seen Frannie, standing on the bottom
step in her dress of many colors and narrowing her eyes at the
jump-rope girls.

The front door was propped open with a cardboard box
containing several framed photographs and plaques that Jim
recognized. Down the hallway, in his former office, Prof was
cleaning out his desk. "Hey, there, Jim," he said. "I should
have done this months ago. You on your way to future fame
and fortune this a of m?"

Jim grinned at his old friend. "I'm on my way somewhere.
You mind if I slip upstairs and say so long to Dr. T?"

"I don't mind and it wouldn't matter if I did," Prof said. "Congrats again on your scholarship. Hit 'em hard, son."

They shook hands and Jim went on down the dim hall and upstairs to the science room. *Thanks, Dr. Templeton. Thanks for your school.* Later, Jim wasn't sure whether he'd spoken the words aloud or just thought them.

Jim continued along the upper corridor from the science lab to his favorite room in the Academy. The library smelled excitingly of well-read old books. On the lectern next to the librarian's desk sat Pliny's wonder-book. Jim began to page through the manuscript. It occurred to him that he might be doing this to put off his departure from the village.

On some pages Pliny had drawn a line through a sentence or paragraph. Here and there he'd inked in a revision. The old headmaster had even made what he'd evidently deemed an improvement to the legend he'd copied from the sounding board above the pulpit. The first three lines, written in the same jet-black ink as the rest of the manuscript, remained unaltered:

> *The Board casts the Dominie's voice on high.*
> *But should that Cleric tell a lie,*
> *The Hand of God lets go.*

The last two lines—"The Board descends on the man below. The Dominie dies"—had been struck out, then revised in blue ink, to read:

> *The Board splits apart on the pulpit below.*
> *There end all lies.*

To Jim the revision seemed out of sync with the rest of the legend. "There end all lies" was less momentous than "The Dominie dies."

"See Genealogy," Pliny'd written in the margin beside the revised lines. But all that remained of the genealogy at the end of the bound manuscript was a jagged strip of paper where the page had been torn out of the book. Why? Why, for that matter, would "all lies end" if the sounding board were to shatter apart on the pulpit of the church? There was a way to find out.

In those years in God's Kingdom, no church door was ever locked. A church was a sanctuary. If a member of the congregation needed to go there to pray, no matter the hour of the day or night, the church needed to be open. If a traveler came through town, even a hobo or a bindle stiff off the railroad, the church door must be unlocked.

The eight-foot stepladder used to dust the woodwork around the tall windows stood on the bottom landing of the belfry, where it was kept when not in use. In the cabinet under the sink of the basement kitchen, Jim located a claw hammer. The ladder and hammer should be all he needed.

A layer of dust coated the top of the sounding board and the carved hand gripping the brass handle. To Jim there was still something deeply disturbing about the Hand of God. He was tempted to smash the thing to bits with his hammer.

Instead, he steadied the wooden box from below with his left hand, wedged the hammer claw under one of the top boards, and began to pry the board upward. The square-headed nails shrieked in protest as they pulled away from the checked pine wood. Jim reached inside the box and felt something smooth. In order to remove it, he had to wrench up another board with the hammer claw.

It was a leather-covered briefcase. Embossed on its side in gold letters were the words "To the Reverend Dr. Pliny Templeton in Commemoration of the Fiftieth Anniversary of the Kingdom Common Academy." Over time, the metal hasps of the case had tarnished, but with a little pressure they snapped open. Inside was a sheaf of papers bound together with a slender cord. They appeared to be the same high-quality vellum as Pliny's manuscript. The elegant, copperplate handwriting was almost certainly the headmaster's.

Jim climbed down the ladder with the briefcase. For some reason he sat in the same place in the second pew he'd sat in three months ago at graduation. He could feel his heart beating faster as he untied the bow knot in the string. In the early sunshine falling through the east windows of the church, Jim read the following letter, addressed to his grandfather.

Good Friday Eve, 1900
Kingdom Common, Vermont

To: James Kittredge Kinneson

My dear James,
    I believe that I may have very little time. I must write quickly. He came at dusk this evening. He will come again tomorrow "before the cock crows thrice." He told me so.

The all-knowing Common will no doubt suppose that we quarreled over my intention to introduce, of all things, a piano into my school. They will imagine that we fought over a minor point of doctrine. Not so, James. The only doctrine your "Kinneson father," as I shall refer to him, ever truly subjected himself to was the doctrine of universal freedom and the total and permanent abolition of all slavery everywhere. In this regard, as has been said of him many times, he "out-Browned John Brown." Yet the great irony, and this you must never forget, is he also has always had only your best interest, and the best interest of your descendants, in mind. He loves you as much as any true father could ever love a child. Where he and I are at variance is whether it is in your best interest to know what I believe I must now tell you, and my dear companion and adoptive brother, your Kinneson father, believes as fervently that I must not.

Might I yet flee? Is there still time? There is. I could flee on the Midnight Special to Boston or the Aurora Borealis to Montreal. I will not be aboard either. I have fled enough, James. First from slavery. Then from Andersonville. And always, since coming here to God's Kingdom, from my own identity. I flee no more forever.

The hands of the steeple clock have wings. I must make my disclosures without further preamble.

Her name—I mean the one girl born to your branch of the Kinneson family since Charles Kinneson I settled here—was Mary. Mary Queen of Scots Kinneson. She was the daughter of your Kinneson father, Charles II, and his wife, Eliza Kittredge Kinneson, and died in the Great Fire of '82, five years after you were born.

Now, James, I must tell you that almost from birth, Mary Kinneson was a mystery to everyone. She was much cherished as the first girl in Charles I's family for many generations, and a very loving child at that. There was no animal, tame or wild, that she did not adore. The birds of the air sometimes flew to her, as they did to St. Francis. As she grew older, it became apparent that she was beloved by small children, whom she would entertain by the hour. She sat for days on end with the sick and elderly and comforted anyone in sorrow. Like you, James, she was a superior student. Yet at heart she was a wilding, with her father's, your Kinneson father's, anarchic spirit. It was the injustice in the world that she could not accept. Whereas your Kinneson father devoted his life to opposing slavery, she seemed determined, from an early age, to oppose Him whom she regarded as the architect of all injustice.

She had long red hair and eyes as green as sea glass. She was long of limb, like her father, and well-proportioned, in a womanly way, from her early teens. That, I fear, may have led to her ultimate downfall, and mine. Yet the entire fault for what transpired rests with me, James, not with Mary. I was old enough to be her father. Nay, her grandfather. And I was married. In the eyes of God, and in my own eyes, I was still married to my wife, sold away from me down the river in what now seems like another life.

Why mince words? Suffice it to say that it is far from unheard of for schoolgirls, at an impressionable age, to become infatuated with their teachers, be they men or women, and vice versa. I do not say this in my own defense. I have no defense.

At my invitation, Mary began attending the evening confirmation classes I taught to the youths of my congregation. She who, at sixteen, was already as confirmed in her outspoken atheism as the Pope of Rome in his priestcraft.

On the pretext of correcting her heresies, I catechized her. Oh, Pliny! Self-duped Pliny! You knew precisely what you were doing.

Mary was a gifted artist. This you know. You have seen, many times, her famous mural at the courthouse, The Seven Wonders of God's Kingdom. *In her oils and watercolors she could capture the unique character of a place or a person. I confess to you that I was flattered when she proposed to paint my portrait, to hang in the great front atrium of the Academy.*

No doubt the portrait was, and is, an excellent likeness. In it, however, she had laid a subtle emphasis on my wide nose, full lips, and dark coloration. I do not mean to suggest that the painting is in any way a caricature. To the contrary, it honors its subject. But whereas, in my tenure in Kingdom County, I have done all in my power to divert attention from my race, by ignoring it, the painting, The Reverend Dr. Pliny Templeton, Founder of the Kingdom

Common Academy, *is unmistakably that of a Negro man. What had I expected it to look like? It looked like me.*

Meanwhile, at our confirmation classes, she had a hundred questions. How could a wholly good creator fashion a world so full of iniquity? How could this same omnipotent God allow His children to so torment and slaughter one another? To be sure, I had been well schooled at the seminary in all of the stock answers to those co-nundrums, to which, I fear, there are no humanly under-standable answers. I spoke, eloquently enough I suppose, of free will, of paradoxes, of what it is given to us to know and not to know. I spoke and she smiled.

What more can I say? Our "classes" had begun in January. By March she was with child. Soon she began to show. Our ardor only increased. James, I should have married her. I loved her, as much for her fearless mind as for her strange beauty. I believe that, for all her antic ways, she loved me. Why else would she make the por-trait in the school lobby far more handsome and noble than he who inspired it?

In desperation, I repaired to my friend and adoptive brother, your Kinneson father. I bared my soul to him. I spared myself nothing. I did everything in my power to exculpate Mary. When I finished my shameful account, Charles regarded me for a moment. I knew that he kept, in his desk drawer, his wartime pistol. I thought he might pull it out and shoot me. I half hoped that he would.

Instead, he gave a harsh laugh. "Hoot, brother," he

said. "I cannot claim to be astonished. True, you of all persons should have known better. Then again, a man's a man. Leave the matter in my hands. Only pledge me one pledge. Give me your word that you will never tell another what you have just told me. Will you pledge?"

"Aye," I said. "I give you my word. I pledge never to tell another what I have told you."

Note this well, James. Sly old Pharisee that I was, I pledged nothing, in our compact, about never writing the truth.

Your Kinneson father—soon enough you will learn why I refer to him as such—then set in motion the machinery of an elaborate scheme. Mary he banished to New Canaan, the community of former slaves that he and I established on the Canadian bank of the Upper Kingdom River. And here a strange story takes a turn stranger still.

Some months before Mary's baby was born, Charles's wife, your Kinneson mother, stopped going to church. She no longer came into the Common to market, nor did she call upon, or receive calls from, neighbors. Charles put out word that she was expecting another child. She was, as you know, much younger than him, though by then near the end of her childbearing years. There was a good deal of concern for her. But in due time, and without incident, she brought forth a healthy male child named James Kittredge Kinneson. That, of course, was you. As for Mary, rumors flew. She had left the Kingdom for the art institute in Montreal. She had died in childbirth. In

...t, she took up with a stonecutter from New Canaan, a decent young man, by all accounts, who treated her well.

In this way, James, a few years passed. And then, dear God, came Armageddon, Armageddon in the incarnation of the Ku Klux Klan. It was a Sunday evening, when most of the New Canaanites were at vespers worship. The Klansmen barred the church door and burned out the church and the village. So far as Charles and I could tell, Mary and her stonecutter consort perished in the flames, which quickly ignited the nearby woods and, as you know, eventually destroyed three million acres of borderland forest, not to mention several entire towns and scores of farmsteads in Vermont, New Hampshire, Quebec, and Maine.

James, I must cut this missive short. I plan to leave it, with the genealogy, inside the sounding board at the church, and to amend, in my History, the legend carved onto that board, as a guidepost that I hope will lead you to their discovery. I know of no other stratagem to put these documents in your hands. Were I to come tonight to your home, the home of your Kinneson father, I am certain he would—but there I will not venture. I will add only that had I married Mary, had I not been a part of Charles's plan to deceive the Common, she would not have died. Thus you perceive the terrible consequences, however unintended, of concealing the truth, and will, I hope, understand why it is of such importance to me to reveal the truth to you now.

*Earlier this year it was announced that a great a,
would be built at the mouth of the Upper Kingdom River
supposedly in order to prevent logjams in the mountain
notch upriver. I believe that the true purpose of this struc-
ture is to conceal the site of the burned village of New
Canaan. To render it out of sight and, therefore, out of
mind. It was this development, to further suppress the
truth, that caused me to make up my mind to break my
own long silence. I told your Kinneson father that I intended to do so, and showed him the genealogy that I recently added to my* History. *He begged me to reconsider.
He implored me. He reminded me of my pledge, and said
writing was no different than telling. He went so far as to
warn me that the revelation I intended to make to you
might make me the agent of my own destruction. I would,
he said, become an accessory to my death as surely as if I
had furnished the weapon that killed me.*

*"Why would you care what I reveal, brother?" I said.
"You of all people. Who gave so much of your life, and
nearly all of your fortune, to the abolition of slavery and
the advancement of former slaves. Surely it cannot be the
taint of Negro blood in your family?"*

*"Blood is blood, Pliny. There is no taint. I know who
you are. It is an honor to have your 'blood,' as well as
mine, in the veins of the boy. Already I see in him, and
am much pleased by, the signs of scholarship and bril-
liance that have distinguished your life. What distresses
me is how he and his descendants will be regarded, and
how treated, in God's Kingdom and beyond. I of all*

people? No. You of all people. You, who, after coming here, never once mentioned your own birthright as a Negro. You should know why I wish to shield our descendants from the hatred, scorn, and perhaps, still worse, the fate that befell the New Canaanites and our beloved Mary."

James, it remains for me to tell you one thing more. My final words to you, or to any of our descendants who may discover this letter, have little to do with your ancestry or mine. Much ado has been made, of late, of my accomplishments over the course of my long life. My Academy. My ponderous old History. My Civil War service, and escape from Andersonville. The scholarship recently established in my name at the state university, of which you are the first recipient.

Yet here and now, with perhaps scant hours left to live, I say to you that I would trade each and every one of these worldly attainments—my school, my degrees, my war medals, all, all, all—for the opportunity to present you to your beloved birth mother, Mary Kinneson, and to show her what a fine and promising young man you have become, a son of whom I, and she, could never have been more proud.

> Signed this Good Friday
> midnight by your loving
> father,
> Pliny Templeton

Postscript: Attached is your family genealogy.

GENEALOGY

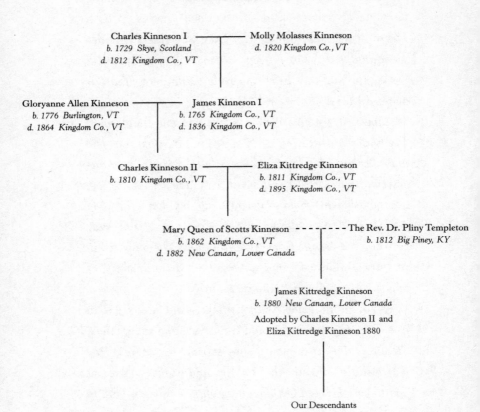

Charles Kinneson I ——————— Molly Molasses Kinneson
b. 1729 Skye, Scotland   d. 1820 Kingdom Co., VT
d. 1812 Kingdom Co., VT

Gloryanne Allen Kinneson ——————— James Kinneson I
b. 1776 Burlington, VT   b. 1765 Kingdom Co., VT
d. 1864 Kingdom Co., VT   d. 1836 Kingdom Co., VT

Charles Kinneson II ——————— Eliza Kittredge Kinneson
b. 1810 Kingdom Co., VT   b. 1811 Kingdom Co., VT
                                  d. 1895 Kingdom Co., VT

Mary Queen of Scotts Kinneson - - - - - - - - The Rev. Dr. Pliny Templeton
b. 1862 Kingdom Co., VT   b. 1812 Big Piney, KY
d. 1882 New Canaan, Lower Canada

James Kittredge Kinneson
b. 1880 New Canaan, Lower Canada

Adopted by Charles Kinneson II and
Eliza Kittredge Kinneson 1880

Our Descendants

On the height of land south of the Landing, just above the
original outlet of Lake Kingdom, Jim pulled off beside the
tall granite obelisk carved with the words "Keep Away." Not
quite a year ago, he'd brought Frannie here to view the pan-
orama of God's Kingdom in its autumn colors. Later, the

height of land became their favorite romantic rendezvous. A few times over the past summer Jim had driven out here, hoping to feel closer to Frannie.

Today a bluish haze hung in the air, a hint of the fall days to come. To the north, the Canadian peaks and the big lake between them were slightly indistinct, though Jim could make out the Île d'Illusion, and the Great Earthen Dam at the mouth of the Upper Kingdom River where, two hundred years ago, his great-great-great-grandfather Charles I had come upon the Abenaki fishing encampment. In the opposite direction, guarding the southeastern entryway to the Kingdom, were the White Mountains of New Hampshire and the long, north-and-south-running crease in the hills of the Upper Connecticut River where Abolition Jim had made his last stand against the federal troops at the second-longest covered bridge in the world. Visible to the west were one hundred miles of the Green Mountains. They, too, had kept God's Kingdom closed off to itself, a territory but little known long after the rest of Vermont had been settled.

"I knew I'd married into a distinguished family," Mom had said after Jim had burst into the newspaper office with the letter from Pliny and the genealogy, and explained what he'd discovered. "I just didn't know how distinguished."

"What should we do with them?" Jim asked his father.

Dad looked at Jim over the top of his reading glasses. "You're the one who found them, son. I'd say it's your call."

Jim hesitated, but only for the briefest moment. "Print them both," he said.

The editor nodded. "Gramp would be proud of you," he said. That was all, but coming from Dad, it meant everything to Jim.

"Now," Dad said, "you've got to get to college and your mom and I have a newspaper to get out. Let's get this show on the road, folks."

High on the ridgetop, Jim looked up the Lower Kingdom River Valley toward the village that had been his home for eighteen years. Already he was homesick. Yet, as he started his truck and headed over the height of land toward the other side of the hills, he knew in his heart that however far he might go, he would always take with him the stories, the mysteries, and the imperishable past of God's Kingdom. For now, that was enough.